CROSS UPS

ANYONE'S GAME

SYLV CHIANG

Art by CONNIE CHOI

annick press
toronto + berkeley

We acknowledge the support of the Canada Council for the Arts and the
Ontario Arts Council, and the participation of the Government of Canada/
la participation du gouvernement du Canada for our publishing activities.

Cataloging in Publication

Chiang, Sylv, author
        Anyone's game / Sylv Chiang ; illustrated by Connie Choi.

(Cross ups ; 2)
Issued in print and electronic formats.
ISBN 978-1-77321-047-6 (hardcover).–ISBN 978-1-77321-046-9 (softcover).–
ISBN 978-1-77321-049-0 (EPUB).–ISBN978-1-77321-048-3 (PDF)

        I. Choi, Connie, illustrator II. Title.

PS8605.H522A82 2018   jC813'.6   C2018-901634-5
                                                C2018-901635-3

Published in the U.S.A. by Annick Press (U.S.) Ltd.
Distributed in Canada by University of Toronto Press.
Distributed in the U.S.A. by Publishers Group West.

Printed in Canada

annickpress.com
connie-choi.com
Follow Sylv Chiang on Twitter @SylvChiang

Also available as an e-book. Please visit www.annickpress.com/ebooks.html for more details.

MIX
Paper from
responsible sources
FSC® C004071

For my mother,
who taught me to stand up for myself,
and
for my fierce daughters.

—S.C.

CHAPTER 1

On screen, my dragon-cross, Kaigo, is locked in battle with Saki, the yeti-cross.

Kaigo breathes fire, but before he can melt the ice off Saki's beard, Saki thrusts a snowstorm my way. The fire extinguishes, and Saki comes in to punish me.

I'm playing my favorite game, *Cross Ups IV.* Kaigo's my main. I play him so much it's like he's a part of me. Not the real me, of course. I'm just a skinny twelve-year-old who's never been in a real fight. Kaigo's the guy I am inside my head.

Kaigo wears kung fu gear and he's totally buff. He's super confident, probably because he can turn into a dragon and blow his opponents' heads off with fireballs.

Most of the time.

Right now, he's being shut down by Saki, who just unleashed a blizzard of punches. The yeti-cross is being played by my friend, Cali. It's the second week of summer holidays and we're playing online.

Cali's gotten good at *Cross Ups* since she moved to live with her dad in Montreal a few months ago. I mean, she was always good, but now she's actually coming close to beating me. I'd better power up.

I go to throw my Dragon Fire Super but she's faster. Her character transforms into a huge yeti and stomps across the screen. Ice flies everywhere. My Health Meter is down to a thin beat of red.

Not cool.

I jump in the air to breathe fire down her neck—a move she never blocks fast enough. But today she does. Before I compute what just happened, a yeti headbutt takes me down.

K.O.

She beat me?

That's not supposed to happen.

Hermlone	Tuesday , 4:08 pm
YES! FINALLY! GTG	

We've been playing for six hours, but I totally don't want to stop. Not on a loss.

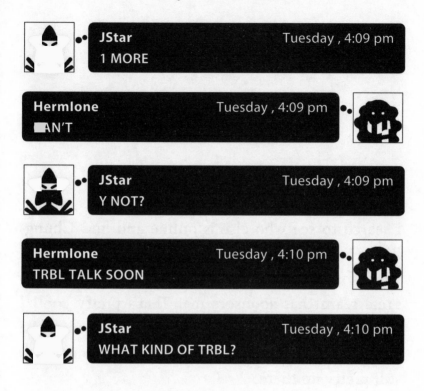

JStar — Tuesday, 4:09 pm
1 MORE

Hermlone — Tuesday, 4:09 pm
█AN'T

JStar — Tuesday, 4:09 pm
Y NOT?

Hermlone — Tuesday, 4:10 pm
TRBL TALK SOON

JStar — Tuesday, 4:10 pm
WHAT KIND OF TRBL?

She logs off before I hit Send.

It's not like Cali to run off just because she finally got a win. Is her dad mad at her for playing so long? Or is it something more serious?

Sometimes Cali's like the yeti. She freezes me out.

CHAPTER 2

I search to see who else is online and find Chung-Key. He's a top-ranked local player for *Cross Ups*. I just found out he's sponsored by ArcadeStix, the same team that sponsors me. That's pretty cool! I mean, he's not as good as my idol Yuudai Sato, the best *Cross Ups* player in the world, but Chung-Key's still pretty up there.

I type an invitation to play, then hesitate. Maybe he won't even know who I am. I see him online all the time but he's never asked me to play. Maybe he thinks I'm some one-hit wonder. I mean, I've only ever gone to one tournament and here I am on his team. He probably doesn't respect me.

Well, the only way to earn respect from gamers is in the game. I hit Send.

WANNA PLAY?

He pings back right away.

OK

I hear my mom coming in the front door with my sister, Melanie. My instincts kick in and I press the off button on my controller.

Ugh, why'd I do that? Now Chung-Key thinks I wussed out.

"*Er zi.*" My mom always speaks to me in Mandarin and calls me that. It means son. "Why are you sitting in the dark? It's a beautiful day."

We've been getting along better lately, and I think part of it is because I've started to speak Mandarin to her. I agree with her. "I was just going to go out."

Melanie smirks, then asks loudly, "What did you do all day? Sit around playing *Cross Ups*?" She can be such a witch.

I ignore her and put on my shoes.

Melanie's working shifts at a golf camp this summer. Mom loves that she's getting fresh air and showing responsibility. But I remember that in past summers she sat around the house doing nothing too.

"Wait," Mom says, putting down a box from the diner where she works. "I brought pie."

The smell of baked apples and cinnamon makes my mouth water. I realize I haven't eaten anything since breakfast. I slip off my shoes and make a detour into the kitchen. "*Xie xie.*" I thank her while I push a quarter of the still-warm apple pie onto a plate and turn to go.

"Sit down and eat properly." Now she's got me. "And answer your sister's question. Did you play video games all day?" I've only been allowed to play *Cross Ups* for about two months now. I used to have to keep it a big secret. Mom's super strict about violent stuff. I guess she thought playing violent games would bring out the gangster in me.

Turns out I don't have any gangster genes. I follow rules (well, most of them) and I'm scared to go out by myself at night. I'm not even close to cool. Mom can stop worrying about gangs recruiting me.

Still, I know she doesn't want me gaming all day, so I cover. "I talked to Cali."

"How's she doing?"

"Fine," I say between bites.

"How's the baby? Does she like being a big sister?"

"Um . . . we didn't exactly get into that."

"Were you too busy telling Cali how much you *love* her?" Melanie calls from the living room.

Mom ignores her. "Is she getting along with her dad and his girlfriend?"

"Yeah, everything's fine." That's probably true. I mean, she didn't mention any problems. Unless that's what *TRBL* meant.

"And you played lots of *Cross Ups* too, I bet." *Shut up, Melanie.*

I'm not sure this pie was worth the interrogation. To shut it down, I shove the rest of the slice into my mouth in one huge bite—Mom doesn't like me to talk with my mouth full.

I'm getting up from the table when the doorbell rings. It's my friend Hugh. Even though he's almost thirteen, his dad makes him go to day camp. He comes to my place every day after camp ends. Today he's got our buddy Devesh with him.

From the hall, Hugh can see into the kitchen. "Hi, Mrs. Stiles." He turns to me. "Dude, what kind?" He's pointing to the pie on the table. As if the flavor matters to him.

"Later," I say and push them toward the porch. I really don't want Hugh talking to my mom. The last thing I need is for her to find out about camp.

"Hi, Hugh. Hi, Devesh." Mom switches to English but pronounces their names *Hoo* and *Dee-vesh*. "You want pie?"

I shake my head at them and mouth *please*.

They pretend to misunderstand. "Yes, please." They take off their sneakers and push past me into the kitchen.

Mom plates two slices. "What you boys do all day?"

The less they say, the better, so I answer. "Devesh just sleeps all day." I'm only partly joking. Since summer holidays started, he's been sleeping in and showing up here later and later. Today, it's after four.

Devesh wrinkles his forehead so his monobrow turns into a squiggle. "Not true. I got up at noon. Would've been here sooner, but I dropped by STEM Camp to see Hugh's catapult in action."

Crap!

"What camp?"

Hugh knows where this is going. Having an over-protective parent is a bond we share. "Oh, it's really boring, Mrs. Stiles. I wish I never signed up."

Devesh's family is different. He's the youngest, with three older sisters, and he's mega-spoiled. His parents would never sign him up for anything he didn't want to do. He doesn't see the warning signs. It only takes one sentence for him to totally ruin my summer. "At least Mr. E's teaching it."

It's a good thing I don't actually have Kaigo's powers, because I'd totally breathe fire on Devesh now.

"The math teacher?" Mom loves Mr. Efram and thinks he's the best teacher ever because he helped me deal with some bullies last year. I admit he's kind of cool. But not cool enough to give up my freedom.

Hugh tries to save me. "I think it's full already." That's a lie. He told me there are only six other kids there.

"I will call and see."

CHAPTER 3

"JStar!" Mr. Efram smiles as I walk into the classroom the next morning. A cool thing about Mr. E is that he's a gamer. A not-so-cool thing is that he calls me by my gamertag now. "Glad you decided to join us. I guess Hugh's told you all about STEM Camp."

STEM stands for Science, Technology, Engineering, and Math. Besides Hugh there are a bunch of younger kids. The website says the camp is for ages eight to twelve. I'm pretty sure the other kids are all eight.

"Hey, Mr. Efram," I say, and slump into the chair next to Hugh. The camp doesn't run out of Mr. Efram's usual math classroom. This is the special education room, which has round tables instead of desks and an air conditioner in the window that sounds like a monster truck.

"Today we're going to solve another science problem together. Who remembers the five steps to 'Get AHEAD' with the scientific method?"

OMG, this is almost exactly the way he started every math class. Except instead of the superhero poster with math problem-solving steps, this poster has Einstein thinking about the scientific method. I put my head on the table while a little kid with a Ninja Turtles shirt says, "AHEAD: Ask, Hypothesize, Experiment, Analyze, Decide."

I close my eyes and think about lucky Devesh, at home, asleep.

◄○►

"How many weeks did your mom sign you up for?" Hugh asks me at lunch.

"The whole month." Fortunately, STEM Camp only goes till the end of July.

"Sorry, dude," Hugh says. "At least I've got someone to hang out with now."

The morning sucked. After working out a boring question about the forces acting on a rocket at the moment of launch, things momentarily looked up when we went outside and launched actual water-bottle rockets. Ours flew up really high, but came straight back down. On my head.

"It'll be nice not being the only unsporty guy from our grade in the gym this afternoon."

"Gym?"

"Yeah, after lunch we join up with the Sports Leadership Camp."

"Tell me you're joking."

—◄○►—

Twenty minutes later we're helping Mr. Efram set up badminton nets. My head's still throbbing.

"Tell me again why we're here," I say to Hugh when Mr. Efram goes into the equipment cupboard.

"Every day Mr. E teaches about the science of a different sport."

"What's that supposed to mean?"

"Basically, whatever science thing we do in the morning, we apply it to sports in the afternoon. Yesterday we did angles and then used it to improve our basketball shots."

"Did it work?" I ask.

"I get the theory, but my shot still sucks."

"This whole camp sucks."

Mr. Efram comes back with a bucket full of

rackets. Hugh pushes his glasses up his nose and whispers, "Dude, I haven't even told you the worst part yet."

The gym doors open and the Sports Leadership Camp kids spill in, laughing and jumping on each other. I recognize two pretty girls from school: Hailey and Tanaka. Is that what Hugh meant? We're going to embarrass ourselves in front of the popular girls. That's nothing new.

But I see the worst part when the last two boys strut through the door.

You've got to be kidding me. These guys are in a leadership camp? They're never going to lead anything, except maybe the local motorcycle gang.

"Look, *Huge* got Jaden to join Loser Camp," Ty says.

"Not on my team," Flash says, fast as the lightning streak shaved into his hair.

◄◦►

Ty and Flash—who probably don't understand any of the lesson about force Mr. Efram does with the group—have no problem using all their *force* to smash birdies at Hugh and me all afternoon. It's more like a game of dodgeball than badminton.

And they make sure Hailey and Tanaka notice every hit by laughing like stupid apes. They're practically pounding their chests.

When we get to my place after camp, Devesh is already there. He's sitting on the swing in front of Cali's front door. Her house is attached to mine and we share a front porch. Of course, she's not home—no one is these days.

I remember the day her mom broke her leg and the paramedics carried her down our shared front steps to the ambulance. Mrs. Chen is still at the rehab center. It's not just the broken leg that's the problem. She has this disease called multiple-something that makes it hard for her to walk. Plus it makes her really tired. Cali had to take care of her a lot last year. Now she's living with her dad until her mom can make it up the stairs and move back home. I know she's worried she might never get to move back here if her mom can't handle it.

Their place has been empty for more than two months, but you can't tell. My mom planted flowers in the Chens' garden, and my dad makes my brother, Josh, cut their grass when he cuts ours. I slump down next to Devesh.

"How long till Cali gets back from Montreal?" Hugh asks, squishing himself between Devesh and me.

"She's supposed to come visit us so she can be closer to her mom," I say, "but I don't know when."

"Probably August," Devesh answers.

"How do *you* know?" Hugh asks.

"I played online with her all afternoon."

Guess she didn't miss me today.

"She's lit," he continues. "The way she plays, I'd never guess she's a girl. I mean, she's even better than that time we played with her in the spring."

I hope she didn't tell Devesh she beat me yesterday.

"Isn't it boring for her to play you?" Hugh says.

"I did okay," Devesh says.

"You beat her?" Hugh asks.

"Once."

"Respect." Hugh gives Devesh a high five.

I interrupt their celebration. "Let me guess—she was playing Cantu?"

"How'd you know?"

"Lately she's been trying new characters. Cantu's the one she's worst at. She was using you to practice."

"I don't mind," Devesh says.

"Yeah, Devesh will do *anything* for Cali." Hugh rolls his eyes.

Devesh shrugs. "So, I think she's pretty."

I never told Hugh and Devesh that Cali kissed me before she left for Montreal. I mean, it was only on the cheek, and it probably didn't mean anything. I don't need these guys bugging me about Cali any more than they already do. It's not like that. She's just a friend.

So why am I mad that Devesh is crushing on her?

CHAPTER 4

Devesh streams a bunch of my matches. He's actually a really good commentator. But he gets the most viewers when Hugh joins him on the mic because Hugh doesn't take it seriously—he just acts like a total goof. Today he's pretending to have a weird accent, like he's in a Shakespeare play.

"This be-eth not a fair pairing," he sneers.

Devesh explains. "JStar's taking on some noob he found online."

"I think-eth he look-eth to increase-eth his standing."

"Yup, and look at that! He perfects the guy!"

"You mean-eth his Health Meter is intact at the end of the round?"

"Exactly. Thank you, Hugh." I don't know how Devesh keeps a straight face.

When they have to go, I keep playing. Mom's working the dinner shift and Dad and Josh are at practice, so I'm eating leftover noodles in the living room and looking for Cali online. She's not there.

I scroll through the names of players, looking for Yuudai Sato. I'd never have the guts to play him, and it's probably the middle of the night in Japan, where he lives, but I always look.

I get an invite from VoldemorT. Who the heck is that? Got nothing else to do, so I accept.

I've had my new ArcadeStix controller for two months now. The company recently sponsored me, which means they gave me this controller and they want me to compete at tournaments and represent them using it.

The thing is huge—bigger than my lap. And it's beautiful—red with the *Cross Ups* logo on it. It's got a stick on the left and six buttons on the right, laid out perfectly for my fingers. The top row of buttons is for punching—light, medium, and hard. The bottom row is for kicks. It's like playing a real arcade game in my living room. I love it!

It took a while to master. You have to practice, like learning to play the piano—except way more fun. I spent the first month in training mode,

perfecting my Dragon Fire Super, until I had the
timing down perfect. But tonight I'm off my game.

And VoldemorT is loving it. He's playing Saki,
and he's good. Icicles fly from his beard and slice
my arms. I try the Dragon Fire Super, but Kaigo
just jumps up and spins around. No dragon. No fire.
Definitely not super.

Saki throws snowball after snowball. They smash
me in the head, the knees, the gut. This is the slowest
possible way to kill me. It's like he's taunting me.

K.O.

If I had a confidence meter, it would be empty.
I can't stop thinking about how Cali beat me. And
when I overthink things, I choke.

I grab another forkful of noodles and press Start to get back to business.

VoldemorT messages me: *HEADSET*

Who is this guy and why does he want to talk? He's probably not going to say anything nice. I consider a rage quit, then decide to suck it up. I grab my headset and hear a girl's voice. Do not tell me I'm getting my butt kicked by another girl.

"Are you letting me win?"

Wait, that's not just any girl's voice. "Cali?"

"Didn't you know it was me?"

"Why'd you change your tag?" I ask. She used to be HermIone.

"Just wanted something different." The wobble in her voice tells me there's more to it than that, but I don't get to ask her because the phone rings.

It's Kyle Obren, the guy from ArcadeStix.

I put Cali on mute.

"How are things, JStar?" he asks.

"Good," I say.

"You've been playing a lot, eh? Your numbers are lookin' hot." He's talking about my stats. I've moved up in the standings since summer break started. Of course, now with stupid STEM Camp I'll probably drop back down.

"Thanks. I've been working at it." Kyle told me to play three hours a day. I was playing around eight most days last week.

"Listen, big news. You know Lance? Sir Lancelot?"

"Sure." I mean, I've heard the name.

"Anyways, he can't make it to the Underground Hype tournament. ArcadeStix is hoping you can fill in. Any chance your parents will go for it?"

Underground Hype! "That's in Montreal, right?"

"Yup. We'll pay train fare. And obviously the entrance is already covered."

"When?"

"This weekend, man."

I'm in hit-stun.

"Want me to talk to your parents?" Kyle asks when I don't say anything.

"No, I got this." I sound way more confident than I feel. "Can you send me the deets?"

"Of course. But listen, I need an answer ASAP. If you can't go, we're gonna send the next guy on our list."

"Okay. I'll let you know." I should be worried about how to get my parents to agree to this, but all I can think is: *I'm not the last person on their list!*

◄o►

"I guess my dad would let you stay here," Cali says when I tell her the news.

This is weird. Isn't she excited for me to visit? "Well, I have to convince my parents first."

"Okay. Let me know." She doesn't sound like she cares either way.

"Everything okay?" I ask.

"What do you mean?"

Good question. "I don't know. Yesterday you said something about trouble." I hold off pressing Start for the next game. I don't want to give her an excuse not to answer. After a while I say, "You still there?"

"Yeah."

"So . . . ?"

"So."

Look, I'm not great at knowing what to say. But she's not helping.

Last try. "Everything's okay?"

"I'm just tired. The baby makes it hard to sleep."

That makes sense, I guess.

CHAPTER 5

"Any chance your parents will let you go?" Hugh asks the next morning at STEM Camp.

"I haven't asked yet. Our calendar says my mom's scheduled to work this weekend and my dad's at a basketball tournament with Josh." My brother is an all-star at, like, *every* sport, and our dad coaches a lot of his teams.

"Even if you can stay with Cali, they probably won't let you take the train alone." Hugh sighs.

"That's why I haven't asked yet. I'm still trying to think of the best way to spin it."

Ironically, today's lesson is all about spin. This can't be good. The only sports link I can think of is throwing a spiral in football, and I'm pretty sure Ty and Flash will be more interested in tackling than throwing.

No surprise, Mr. Efram starts off with the Einstein "Get AHEAD" poster again. He's got a bucket of water on the table next to him. "*A* is for *ask*. Today we ask the question, What will happen if I swing this bucket of water in a big loop over my head so the bucket goes upside down?"

"Probably nothing exciting," I whisper to Hugh.

"Mr. Stiles! You have a hypothesis to share for *H*?"

Ugh. "I think the water will stay in the bucket."

"What makes you think that?"

"Well, you don't have a mop."

"Fair enough." Mr. Efram winks at me and points back to the poster. "*E* is next, for *experiment*. Let's see what happens." He picks up the bucket and spins it quickly in big circles up and over his head.

"Now *A*. Let's *analyze* our data," he says. "What did you observe?"

"The water stayed in," a kid in the front row yells. "Not even one drop came out—I was watching!" He sounds way too excited.

"So, time for *D. Decide*. Was Jaden's hypothesis correct?"

Everyone, including Hugh, calls, "Yes."

"So, I can be sure that the next time I spin a

bucket of water over my head, the water will stay in, right?"

Hugh's hand shoots up. "It depends how fast you spin it. If you go too slow, there won't be enough force to hold the water in the bucket."

"Thank you, Hugh, for that new hypothesis. But let's go outside this time."

After Mr. Efram dumps the bucket of water on his head, we head back to class and spend the morning spinning things like pennies, tops, and eggs. I have to admit, I'm surprised that hard-boiled eggs are easier to spin. But when Hugh spins a raw one off the table I'm happy to take a break—time to find the caretaker.

As we pass the gym, we stop to peek at the sports camp through the window in the gym doors. They're running lines: you run to touch a line, run back, then run to touch the next line, over and over again. I can't stand that drill—it's exhausting. No wonder those kids are all in better shape than us.

Ty is gaining on the guy next to him. By the time he finishes, his teammate, Flash, takes off at the same time as the other team's last runner. As his nickname suggests, Flash is the fastest kid in our grade. His real name is William or Willard or something.

I start to walk away.

"Dude, check this out," Hugh calls after me.

Flash hasn't pulled away at all. He's running line for line with his competitor—Hailey.

I'm glued to the window with Hugh. "No way! Flash is going to lose to a girl!"

They're moving in sync, dipping together at each line, like dancers doing a routine.

"They'll need a replay to figure out who wins," Hugh says.

At the fifth of six lines, Flash stops dipping down. He just touches the line with his foot and moves on.

The milliseconds he saves by skipping the last dips is enough to put him in the lead at the finish.

"Cheater," we both mutter as we head off to find the caretaker.

—◄o►—

As I predicted, that afternoon we head outside to the football field. Mr. Efram makes Hugh and me team captains, probably to save us the embarrassment of being picked last over little kids and girls.

I don't want Ty or Flash, so I pick Hailey first. At least I know she's fast.

Major miscalculation.

"Aww! Jaden loves Hailey!" Ty calls while Flash makes kissing sounds. The younger kids join in and everyone laughs except Hugh, Tanaka, and Hailey.

Now Hugh's up. He can't pick Tanaka after that scene, so he points to the biggest kid from Sports Leadership Camp.

Each person selected is in charge of picking the next person.

Hailey picks Tanaka, obviously. In the end, because no one else wants to be called out for being in love, my team is mostly girls and Hugh's is all guys, including Ty and Flash.

Coach Lee gives instructions for throwing a spiral and tells us to practice in our teams on separate halves of the field.

"So, the *girls'* team is on that side, right, Mr. E?" Ty says, just to be a jerk.

Fortunately, all the hours of "boy time" hanging out with my dad and my all-star brother gave me one skill: I can throw a decent spiral.

Unfortunately, the kid I'm tossing to, the last boy picked, can't catch. Plus he keeps overthrowing, so I have to run and get the ball every time. We look like a disaster.

Across the field, Hugh has strategically paired himself with a little kid so he has an excuse to stand close and throw lightly. He looks like a nice big brother. No one would know he can't throw any better than his six-year-old partner.

Next to him, Ty and Flash are showing off. They've spread out twice as far as everyone else. Ty jumps up to catch the ball and lands hard, rolling across the pitch clutching it to his chest. When he stands up, he looks at Hailey and Tanaka, spikes the ball, and does a funky chicken dance, his arms out like wings while his feet do the running man.

The girls roll their eyes.

My partner hits Hailey in the shoulder with the ball. Ugh.

"Sorry," I say. We both bend to pick up the ball at the same time and bump heads. I say "Sorry" again, and she looks at me. Are her eyes green or gray? I can't stop looking at them.

"He's trying," I say, pointing to my partner.

"No worries," she says.

I hesitate, then add, "Flash totally cheated today."

She stares at me. I swear I've never seen eyes that color before.

"When you guys were racing."

"What?" she asks. Now I realize it sounds creepy, like I was spying on her or something.

"Uh, we were passing the gym when you guys were running lines."

"Okay . . ."

"You totally had him." *Shut up, Jaden. You sound like a fanboy.*

"Yeah, I know," she says, like I just told her footballs aren't round.

Awkward.

CHAPTER 6

Coach Lee says captains are the quarterbacks. That means me and Hugh will be the ones deciding who to throw the ball to while everyone else does the running. I'm happy because I can finally prove that I can throw. Hugh's happy because he won't have to run.

Our team huddles up. Everyone talks at once, but they eventually pick positions.

Ty and Flash dominate their team's offense. Plus, they cheat. Whenever someone tags them, they yell, "No! No! You never touched me. I didn't feel it!"

When we're on offense, my strategy is simple: throw to Hailey.

I'm nervous, so my first throw is a bit wobbly. She reaches for it, but it goes off her fingertips.

My next throw is good, but she gets tripped up by a little science kid from the other team who's sitting on the field picking dandelions.

Before the third play, Ty yells, "He's passing to Hailey again. Flash, stay on her."

I look at Hailey, wondering if I should throw to someone else.

She nods to say she can take him.

Hailey moves down the line to get away from Flash. He scrambles to follow, chasing her across the field. No one's near them. No one else is fast enough. I heave the ball and send a perfect spiral to exactly where Hailey ends up. She turns at exactly the right second, catches the ball, and races down the field. I see it all in slow motion, like a *SportsCentre* replay. Her ponytail flows in the wind behind her as she gallops toward the end zone.

If that beautiful play didn't make the highlight reel, what happens next definitely would.

When Hailey slowed down to catch the ball, Flash gained on her. As they near the goal line, she's just barely out of his reach.

I don't know if he's still mad that Hailey almost beat him today, or if he's just used to cheating, but Flash leaps at Hailey and takes her down with a full-on tackle at the line.

Coach Lee blows the whistle.

Flash dances away, leaving Hailey in the grass.

What a jerk. Everyone knows you ease up on a girl.

When we get back to my place, Devesh is waiting on the porch again. I tell him about Montreal. "Awesome!" he says. "I'll go with you!"

Hugh punches him in the shoulder. "You just want to see Cali!"

He turns to Hugh. "That's a bonus. You should come too. It'll be epic!"

"Her dad is never going to let us all stay there," I say. "They have a new baby."

"No problem. I have an uncle in Montreal we can stay with. We were there last summer for my cousin's wedding. It's a huge house. They packed, like, eighteen people in there that week. And, since my cousin got married, her room must be free now. They can fit the two of us, no problem. And you too, if Cali's dad says no."

This just might work. "Maybe . . ." While the guys play *Mega Haunt*, I spend the next hour planning exactly what to say when I plead my case to Mom.

But Devesh totally messes up my plans. Mom hasn't even put her purse down when he says, "Mrs. Stiles, great news! Jaden's got a tournament this weekend in Montreal."

"What?" She looks from Devesh to me.

"I'll tell you about it later," I say. This is *so* not the right time. When she gets home from work she's always busy and stressed. I was planning to ask her after dinner.

"It's okay, Mrs. Stiles. We're all going together. So it'll be very safe." I know he thinks he's helping by mentioning safety, but I'm pretty sure he's having the opposite effect.

"What? You boys want go to Montreal *alone*?"

"Not alone. Together." Devesh throws his arms over Hugh's shoulder and mine.

"Don't you guys have to go home?" I say.

Hugh squishes a laugh. "C'mon, dude. You're messing everything up." He tugs Devesh's T-shirt as he gets up off the couch.

Devesh follows Hugh reluctantly. "What'd I do?"

In the kitchen, I start setting the table to gain some points. I need every advantage I can get if I'm going to win this battle.

"What was he talking about, *er zi*?"

Stupid Devesh. There's no putting this off now. I summon Kaigo and make my first move. I speak Mandarin to get on her good side. "There's a tournament, and the team *needs* me to go." I picked the word *needs* earlier. It sounds like I have to go. Next, I push the positive. "The good thing is, it's in Montreal, so I can stay with Cali." Hopefully.

"Montreal is too far. You cannot go there without us. When is it?"

As soon as I tell her, she says no.

I don't give up. Kaigo won't let me. He throws a jab. "Devesh and Hugh will go with me."

"No."

We take some damage, but Kaigo shakes it off and tries an uppercut. "You could put us on the train and Cali's dad will meet us at the other end. We'll be fine."

"No. You're twelve. I'm not sending you without an adult."

We're on the ground in hit-stun. Adult? Wait. Kaigo jumps up from the ground in that funky back-arch way that only martial artists and break-dancers can do. He throws a desperation side kick. "There are adults on the team. I can travel with them." Maybe? I've never talked to them before, but I could ask.

"No. I don't know these people."

I'm out of moves.

K.O.

CHAPTER 7

When Mr. Efram points to the stupid "Get AHEAD" poster the next morning, I make a little mouth out of my hand and mock him behind his back while he reads out the steps.

"Ask," say Mr. Efram and my hand.

"Hypothesize." I wobble my head while I move my fingers open and closed.

"Experiment." The little kids giggle now but I just glare at them.

Then Mr. Efram pauses, so my hand moves but no words come out. Without turning around he asks, "Would your puppet like to tell us the last step, Jaden?"

How'd he do that?

"Decide," I mumble.

Today's project is something about balancing sticks with marshmallows on the ends to find the center of gravity. I eat three marshmallows while Hugh sets up our sticks.

Mr. Efram pulls up a chair next to me. "Everything okay, JStar?"

I don't want to have this conversation. "Yeah," I say.

"You seem a bit off." He's not leaving.

I look at Mr. Efram. He's an adult. My parents trust him. I wonder . . .

"Any chance you're going to the Underground Hype tournament in Montreal this weekend?" I ask. Hugh's head whips around.

"No. Are you?"

"Supposed to, but my parents are busy."

"That explains the attitude this morning."

I drop my head to the desk. I don't know what I was expecting. Like he's going to offer to come with me. Asking him would sound so stupid.

I get a chance to hear exactly how stupid when Hugh says, "Could you take us—I mean, Jaden—to the tournament? He needs a responsible adult."

Mr. Efram smiles long enough to give me hope. "Sorry, guys, I've got plans this weekend." He might as well just punch me in the face.

◄○►

Mr. Efram and Coach Lee set up balance beams, benches, and even a slack line—this strip of stretchy material that's basically like a tightrope.

"Today, your job is to navigate the gym without touching the ground. Use your arms to help you balance," Mr. Efram says.

Coach Lee blows his whistle. "Let's go!"

Hugh sighs. This is not his kind of activity. Neither of us is sporty, but he really sucks at climbing and balancing. He swings his leg up to get onto the first beam and Flash calls out, "Brace yourselves! *Huge* is getting on." What a jerk.

Hugh puts his foot back on the floor.

"Leave him alone," I say.

"Or what?"

Good question. If we were in *Cross Ups*, I'd show him what. But here in the gym, if I could ever catch him, I'd be the one getting my butt kicked.

Since I can't hurt him physically, I shame him like he did to Hugh. "Whatever. You're a fraud. Hailey would have totally beaten you yesterday running lines if you actually followed the rules."

Hailey passes on a beam above us. Her green-gray eyes say *Don't get me involved in your issues.*

Ty jumps in to defend his friend. "Shut up. You know he's the fastest guy in our grade."

"Exactly. The fastest *guy*!" I look up at Hailey, but she's already on the next beam.

Ty goes in for the kill. "You like her, don't you?"

When I don't answer right away, he screams, "I knew it!"

"I don't," I say, but I know it sounds like I do. I mean, don't we all like her? She's pretty and athletic and . . . everything.

"Jaden has a girlfriend already." I know Hugh's trying to help, but who's going to believe that? "In Montreal."

"Oh yeah? And I have a girlfriend in Boston. And one in Florida," Ty says.

Flash adds, "And don't forget the one in Tampa Bay." Idiots. They're totally just naming NHL teams.

"No, really. Her name's Cali." *Shut up, Hugh.*

This shaming thing is not working out the way I planned. I've got to turn this around. "It's not about that. It's about how you're cheaters."

"We don't cheat."

"What about yesterday when you tackled Hailey because you couldn't tag her." That'll show them.

"Hailey again! You can't stop talking about her."

I lose it and scream, "You. Tackled. A. Girl!"

"She tripped." Flash is in my face now. The last thing I need is to get into a fight. There's no way my mom would let me go to the tournament after that. She'd probably never even let me play *Cross Ups* again.

But I know I'm right. "Everyone knows you're supposed to ease up on a girl. Didn't your mom teach you manners?"

While we've been arguing, Hailey has gone around the entire circuit. She's back on the beam next to us and I look up, proud of the way I defended her honor.

For some reason, she doesn't look at me like her knight in shining armor. She just jumps down, shakes her head, and walks away.

Tanaka says, "You guys are all idiots."

"Good news! My uncle's expecting us. Just tell your parents that my dad's coming along," Devesh says when he hears how things went down with my mom.

"Is he?"

"No way—he can't stand my uncle. But your mom doesn't have to know that." Devesh flops on my couch and grabs the controller to turn on my gaming system.

"She'd want to talk to your dad about the arrangements. She'd probably want to show him how my puffer works."

"Just think about it, okay? It's your only chance."

He's right. It's Thursday already. If I'm going, I have to leave tomorrow afternoon. Ugh! Does getting to tournaments always have to involve lying to my mom?

Devesh scrolls through the list of players online.

"She changed her gamertag," I say.

"I know." Is it just me, or does Devesh sound cocky?

"What'd she do that for?" Hugh asks. "She's got a good ranking."

"Dunno. Said she wanted a change. She's VoldemorT now."

"VoldemorT? Like the bad guy from *Harry Potter*?" Hugh pulls a face.

"Maybe she wants people to know she's badass," Devesh says.

"Hermione's badass," Hugh says.

"No comparison. Hermione's a goody-goody girl. Voldemort's an evil wizard who kills people for revenge. There she is." Devesh clicks on VoldemorT. She's already playing someone.

While I'm in the kitchen grabbing chips, Melanie comes home with her boyfriend. Roy's cool. Not sure what he sees in Melanie.

He takes my spot on the couch while she runs upstairs to shower. "Hey guys. Anyone beat Jaden lately?"

"Yeah, Cali did!" Devesh says. *She told him?*

"Oh yeah?"

"Just once," I say, opening the bag of salt and vinegar. "I was having a bad game."

"It's good to lose once in a while," Roy says, reaching into the bag. "Keeps it real."

I sit on the coffee table. We pass the bag and munch chips. Hugh gives me a little wave and points to Roy. Then he mouths something I can't make out.

What? I mouth back.

"Adult," he coughs, flicking his head at Roy.

He's right. Roy's eighteen and going to university in September.

Devesh is looking at us. I'd better jump on this before he ruins it. "You working this weekend?"

Roy works at the diner with my mom. "No."

"Any plans?"

"Just hanging out with Mel."

"Any chance you want to go to Montreal?"

He looks at me sideways and I explain the situation.

"Mel will kill me if I take off for the weekend without her."

"And Mom will never let you guys go away together." I sigh.

"Why can't Mel take you?"

I snort.

If Melanie is my only hope, it's not happening. I should have known going to Underground Hype was too good to be true.

CHAPTER 8

"Cali's finally done," Devesh says, clicking on VoldemorT to start a match. He grabs the headset from the table and talks into the mic. "Took you long enough." After a pause, he says, "C'mon. Just a couple games." Another pause. "Why not?" Pause. "Okay." He hands me the headset. "She wants to talk to you."

I put the headset on. "Cali? What's up?"

"I don't feel like playing anymore. Can you please get Devesh to drop it?" Her voice sounds wobbly again.

"Yeah, no problem." I walk into the kitchen and close the door. "You okay?"

"Yeah . . ."

I wonder if this has something to do with her mom. "I don't believe you. What's going on?"

"My dad said it's okay if you stay here this weekend."

"Oh. That's good, if—"

"Can you?" There's that wobble in her voice again.

"I don't know. I've got one last hope."

Her voice is small. "Please."

I get a funny feeling, like an electric jolt running through my body. That must be why I say the stupidest thing possible. "I'll be there."

—◦—

At dinner it's just me, Melanie, and Mom because Dad and Josh already left for their out-of-town basketball tournament.

Roy must have some video game superpowers over Melanie. I feel like *Cross Ups* is happening right in my kitchen. Just like Kaigo transforms into a dragon in *Cross Ups*, I watch a real-life dragon transform into a caring big sister.

"I'd feel so bad if Jaden missed out on going to his dream tournament, wouldn't you, *Ma ma*?" Melanie says in Mandarin. She never speaks Mandarin to Mom.

I'm confused. I've never seen this creature before. But I cover it up by looking really depressed, like Roy told me to.

"I'd be willing to give up my plans to take him to Montreal. I'd love to see how Cali's doing. Maybe she could use some tips from one big sister to another." She sounds phony as hell.

"*Nu er*, that is so generous. But don't you have to work?"

Wait, is Mom buying this?

"I could get someone to fill in for me. Quin's been begging for more hours."

Sometimes parents just see what they want to see. Mom must really want to believe we get along. "Let me give Cali's father a call and see if he's okay with both of you coming." She leaves her dinner to get the phone.

"What's going on?" I hiss.

"What do you mean?"

"Why are you acting like you give a crap about me?"

"I *do* care about you. You're my brother."

"Riiiight. What did Roy say to you?"

"He feels sorry for you." She looks down at her plate. "And he pointed out that maybe I'm not always that nice, and this could be a way to make it up to you. Now you owe me one, right?"

"Fine." I'll take owing Melanie if it gets me to Montreal. Not like I have any other options.

We hear Mom on the phone from the living room. "You sure is not too much trouble?" She speaks English to Mr. Chen because he doesn't know Mandarin.

As soon as Mom hangs up, the phone rings again. It's Kyle. "JStar, what's the word?"

I throw a questioning look at Mom. She nods.

"I'm in."

"Awesome. I'll email you the info package for the tournament. The team meets Saturday morning for breakfast at the hotel. See you then."

This is really happening. I go to my room to print out the forms and do a happy dance.

◄○►

Because I'm not thirteen yet, I need my mom to sign a permission form.

Last time I got invited to a big tournament, I didn't exactly tell her about it when I signed up. I'm glad I don't have to lie this time. Still, I'm kind of nervous about asking her.

I find her in the living room watching the news. There's a report on how crime rates rise in the summer months in big cities. Great, just what I need her to hear. Why couldn't she be watching something funny?

I detour to the kitchen for a snack, and wait for the news story to change to something about wildfires in California. Fire is Kaigo's power. This is a good sign.

I join her on the couch. As usual, I use Mandarin. "*Ma ma*, I need you to sign this." I pass her the paper and the pen I brought.

She reads it over. "Be careful, okay?"

"Of course."

She looks at me. "And listen to your sister."

I nod.

"You guys are growing up so fast. You know, I was your sister's age when I left Taiwan."

I look at my mom and try to imagine her at seventeen. I wonder if she looked like Melanie. "Why did your family move so far?"

"Actually, it was just me and my brother—your Uncle Sammy."

"What?"

"Our parents sent us to live with our dad's sister here so we could go to university in English and get better jobs."

"Why didn't you go back home after you finished school?"

"Going back is not an option. And anyways, soon after graduating I met your dad, and . . . well, this is home now."

CHAPTER 9

Camp doesn't seem as bad Friday morning. The note in my pocket to get out early is like a free pass to skip a torture session. Hugh has a note too. His dad bought the story about Devesh's dad coming along.

When we hand our notes over to Mr. Efram at lunchtime, he smiles. "So, you found a responsible adult?"

"Nah. My sister's taking us."

He laughs. "Well, have fun. But watch your back. The rivalries in the fighting game community are pretty intense."

His warning echoes in my head as we walk down the school hall to the main doors. The Sports Leadership Camp kids are on their way to the lunchroom.

"Where are you girls going?" Ty asks.

"You know, *girl* is not an insult," Tanaka says.

"Sorry. Where are you *geeks* going?" Ty is such a jerk.

"Actually, we're going to Montreal."

Why, Hugh?

"Yeah, right. You going to visit Jaden's girlfriend?" Flash smirks.

Hugh can't help himself. "Yup. J's going to stay at her place and everything."

Does he really think Cali's my girlfriend? Or is he just saying that to shut Ty and Flash up? It's weird. I mean, she's my friend and she's a girl. I like hanging out with her, and I guess she's pretty. Does that make her my girlfriend? Is that why she kissed me?

"Whatever. You guys are so lame," Ty says. "No one believes you."

"Oh yeah? We can prove it," Hugh says. *We can?* "His sponsor's sending him to compete at the Underground Hype tournament. Watch him on Twitch. ArcadeStix will appreciate the views."

That shuts Flash up. Now who's lame?

But Ty isn't done. "Have you heard, Hailey? Jaden's a gamer. Maybe you want to watch him play video games. Isn't that what girls like?"

Hailey rolls her eyes. "You guys have no idea what girls like."

◄o►

Back at my place we grab our stuff and sit on my front steps. We each have a big backpack, but I also have a little black rolling suitcase my mom pulled out of the basement. It has my ArcadeStix controller in it. The thing is so mega. When I tried packing it in my backpack there wasn't room for anything else.

I try to imagine what it's like for Cali at her dad's new place. She doesn't know anyone in Montreal. When she got to her new school there were only two months left before summer break. I wonder if she made any friends. She doesn't even speak French.

There's a sound, and I realize it's my hands hitting the steps. I have this weird habit of tapping my thumbs when I'm nervous, like I'm using a controller. In the world of *Cross Ups*, with a controller in my hands, I can get through any battle. I wish there was a controller that could help me when I don't know what to do in real life—which is, like, always.

"I can't believe we're going to Montreal, dude," Hugh says.

"I know. This is nuts," I say.

"It's going to be amazing, as long as my dad doesn't find out." I don't really like being part of Hugh's lie, but he'd do it for me. And I really want him to come.

Mom pulls into the driveway. I yell through the door for Melanie. She takes forever, and I wonder if we're going to miss the train. When she gets into the passenger seat, the whole car stinks up from her disgusting flowery body spray. Why's she even wearing that? I look closer and note the lacy white halter top and droopy earrings. Who's she dressing up for, the train conductor?

"You guys be careful."

"Yes, Mom."

"Don't talk to strangers."

"We know."

"Listen to your sister."

"Uh-huh."

"Behave at Cali's house."

It goes on like this the whole way to the station. Normally I'd get mad at her for being so momzilla, but I just keep my mouth shut and think about the tournament. There's no way I'm messing this up now.

We find Devesh waiting on the platform.

"You alone?" my mom asks.

"My sister dropped me off," Devesh says. "She was in a rush. Said she had to get back to work, but I think she's really meeting her boyfriend."

"This is a lot of food, Mom," Melanie says, taking the big paper bag my mom brought from the diner.

"You're traveling with three hungry boys," Mom says in Mandarin.

When the train pulls in, Melanie tells us to get on the first car. "It's the safest. If there's an accident, statistically we have the best chance of survival," she says when we ask her why it matters. Who is this weird responsible-big-sister droid? I don't trust it.

When we climb onto the train, Mom takes her worrying to the next level. "Call me when you get there, or if there's a problem. Actually, call me every hour so I know you're still okay."

I wave and move on before she can change her mind and pull me off the train.

It's crowded in the first car. Seats are set up in pairs facing each other, so each section is a group of four. There is already at least one person in every section. Melanie insists we sit down in the three empty seats where an old lady is sitting alone. She

finds a spot a couple of sections over as the train pulls out of the station.

We've just barely gotten seated when we find out the real reason Melanie agreed to come along.

CHAPTER 10

There's a rush of sound when the door between train cars opens.

"Surprise!" Roy announces. "You didn't think I'd miss out on the fun, did you?"

It all makes so much sense now: the outfit, the perfume, the caring-big-sister act. She said I owe her one and here it is. Another lie I'm in on.

Roy gives us high fives then sits with Melanie.

The old lady in our section gives me a dirty look and starts telling me off in French. My frazzled expression and repeated "*Je ne comprends pas*"—the only phrase I've really got down from French class—don't help. Finally, a woman in the section next to us leans over and explains that I am supposed to store my suitcase on the overhead rack.

"Oh, sorry," I say, and maneuver myself out of

my seat. With the lady's huge purse, our three back-packs, and my suitcase, there's hardly room to step. I almost hit the lady with my case as I lift it over her lap.

I'm lucky my case is small. With some squishing, it just fits between two other small black cases. When I sit back down, Devesh is already asleep, leaning against the window. Scared to talk in case the French lady gets mad, we sit in silence, slowly being rocked by the train's rhythmic shake. Eventually Hugh falls asleep too, and I watch a line of drool slide down his chin.

I want to sleep, but I'm freaking out. This is only my second tournament ever. What if I suck this time? I mean, even Cali beat me. And what was Mr. Efram talking about when he said there was intense rivalry between teams? The lady gives me cut-eye whenever my thumbs start tapping, but I can't control them.

I read the info package about the tournament over and over. The rules are almost the same as the ones I memorized before my last tournament. I don't know at what point in the five-hour journey I finally nod off, but when I wake up the train is stopped, my head is on the old lady's shoulder, and her head is on mine.

Roy's shaking me. "C'mon, J. We're here."

Hugh, Devesh, and Melanie are already heading out the door. I grab my backpack and race after them through the big station.

It's only a few minutes later, when someone cuts in front of me and I almost trip over their rolling suitcase that I remember—my suitcase is still on the train!

—◯—

I make everyone run back to the platform at supersonic speed, but it's too late. Our train is gone. My controller is on its way to Quebec City with that stupid old lady.

I want to crumple on the train station floor. I can't compete without a controller. I might as well have left my hands at home. ArcadeStix is so going to drop me.

When we find Cali and her dad I'm so mad I hardly register them.

My imagination takes me to an arena and lets Kaigo beat me up.

How could I be so stupid? Punch to the face.

Why didn't I pay more attention? Leg swipe.

What idiot forgets his most valuable possession on a train? Elbow strike to the chin.

I shake my head and try to focus. Through a haze I see Melanie hug Cali. She explains about my suitcase. Devesh hugs Cali too, and I'm glad to see she backs out of it.

"Aw, c'mon. Don't cry over this," Cali's dad says. That brings me back to reality because, no joke, there's an actual tear running down my cheek. "Can't you just borrow Cali's joystick?"

"It's called a controller, Dad." Cali rolls her eyes. "You can totally use one of mine tomorrow. Don't worry, you did great last time with one just like it."

"Who's picking you up?" Melanie asks Devesh and Hugh. I look around and realize Roy has disappeared.

"We're taking the metro. My uncle lives close to Atwater station." Devesh acts like he's some world traveler. Why can't he just say subway?

Everyone makes plans for meeting tomorrow. I don't see the point. We might as well take the next train home. I watch my friends head toward the METRO sign. Stepping out from behind a pillar, Roy falls in step behind them as they pass through the turnstile.

Cali notices and looks at me with raised eyebrows. I'm still too much of a mess to respond. I'm such a loser.

◄O►

On the car ride home, Melanie calls the railway company's lost and found number, but it's Friday after five o'clock so she gets a recorded message. There's zero chance I'm getting my controller in time for the tournament tomorrow. I might never see it again. I feel like I just got punched in the stomach.

Mr. Chen pulls the car up in front of a tiny bungalow with a red door. From the driveway we can hear a baby screaming.

"Warning, it's the witching hour," Mr. Chen says.

I look at Cali.

"Ruby always cries around dinner time," she says.

"And she doesn't stop until morning," Mr. Chen adds. I can't tell if he's joking.

CHAPTER 11

Mr. Chen's girlfriend, Marnie, greets us with the screaming baby in her arms. I met her when she was pregnant with Ruby, and she still looks about the same, but not nearly as energetic. In fact, she looks like she hasn't slept in a year.

"Hi, Jaden. Hi, Melanie," she says, giving us each a limp hug, which apparently Ruby does not like, since she ramps up the volume. "Sorry, Ruby's colicky."

That's the last we see of Marnie. She spends the next few hours in the bedroom, trying to get the baby to sleep. Whatever she's doing, it's not working.

Inside, the house looks even smaller than it did from the outside. It's like a wizard came by and cast a shrinking spell on a normal house.

The kitchen is cramped and littered with dishes,

mostly baby bottles. How can a little baby drink so much? Cali goes to the cupboard and starts taking out cans of soup. Melanie stops her and pulls out the bag of food Mom sent along. There are noodles, vegetables, and even a whole fish. I don't know how my mom thought we could eat this on the train.

It's enough to feed us all, with leftovers. Mr. Chen takes a plate of food and disappears to the living room to watch TV. Me and Cali sit at the kitchen table with Melanie, who only looks up from her phone to fork food into her mouth.

"Sorry. Things are different here than with my mom," Cali says.

I wonder what she means. The small house? The fact that we're all eating separately? Or the screaming? I don't know what to say so I just smile and chew.

"At least you're here now," she says.

"You think you'll get to come home soon?"

"No. Whenever I ask my mom she says, 'not yet.' And my dad says I need to think of his place as home too. I think he just likes the free help for Marnie. If I wash bottles, it's less work for him."

"Really?"

"I don't know. That's what it feels like. I miss my real home."

After we eat, we head to Cali's room. It takes about three steps to get there from the kitchen. You could cross the entire house in ten.

There's a mattress next to Cali's bed, and it's taking up all the floor space. That's where Melanie will sleep. No one's said where I'll sleep. I'm guessing the bathtub. I hope it's a normal size.

Cali says, "I know, it's small, right?"

"Nah," I lie. Worst is the fact that her room is

next to Ruby's. Does she ever stop crying? I'm so glad I don't live here. Then I spy something that makes me reconsider. "They let you keep your gaming system in your bedroom?"

"There's nowhere else."

We plunk ourselves on her bed and start playing *Cross Ups*. I need to get used to the gamepad controller again, fast.

Melanie lies on the mattress with her phone, probably texting Roy. When Cali shouts *Yes!* after knocking me out, Melanie looks up. "Why didn't *you* sign up for the tournament? I hear you beat Jaden."

Seriously? Does everybody know?

"Not my scene."

"Why not? You obviously love it, and you're really good." Melanie has a point.

"It's more for guys," Cali says. That's true. There aren't many girl competitors. I remember walking around the T3 tournament with Cali and counting only twelve girls in the room, including Cali and my mom.

"So what? You could totally whip their butts." Melanie's voice rises the way it does when she's in the mood for a fight. "Just because there aren't that many girls competing doesn't mean you shouldn't. There aren't a lot of girl golfers either. That hasn't stopped me. It's how I got my summer job. The club owner thinks having a female camp counselor encourages more girls to join the program. I'm a role model! I show that girls play golf too."

"Shut up, Melanie," I say. "Fighting games aren't like golf."

◄o►

My bed for the night is the couch. The living room is way too close to the baby's room. Actually, every room is.

All I have is what's in my backpack: my MP3 player, a hoodie, a half-eaten bag of Oreo cookies, the papers from Kyle, and my toothbrush. My clothes are in the suitcase with my controller, so I'm wearing clothes I borrowed from Cali to sleep in. Thank god Cali doesn't wear girly stuff. She gave me gray drawstring track shorts and a black T-shirt. It's tight, but better than sleeping in my clothes, since I'll have to wear those again tomorrow. And Sunday.

I lie there, trying to figure out what to say to Kyle tomorrow. How am I going to explain that I don't have the controller he gave me? What if he doesn't let me compete? The whole point of ArcadeStix sponsoring me is for me to come out and dominate using their product.

Plus, how bad will I suck using Cali's controller? The arcade stick took some getting used to, but now I hate playing without it. I've gotten so good at throwing all Kaigo's Supers, even Dragon Fire. That one is so hard with a gamepad.

I toss and turn. Between my nerves and the screaming baby, sleep is impossible.

There's light creeping out from under Cali's bedroom door. I peek in. Cali's sitting on the mattress on the floor playing a mirror match: Saki versus Saki.

I flop onto the bed next to Melanie. "I can't believe this," she says.

Neither can I. Melanie cares about gaming? Maybe I did fall asleep and this is some weird dream. "I know, she's good." I yawn.

"That's not what I mean," Melanie says. "Look at those messages."

I look at the screen. Someone's messaging Cali over and over, even though Cali isn't answering.

ShoMe   Friday, 11:40 pm
U WERE HERMIONE

ShoMe   Friday, 11:41 pm
THINK I CANT FIGURE OUT?

ShoMe   Friday, 11:41 pm
FIGHT ME

ShoMe   Friday, 11:42 pm
VOLDMORT 2 HERMIONE—I NO ITS U

ShoMe   Friday, 11:42 pm
SHO U WHAT HAPPENS TO GIRLS WHO PRETEND

I shrug. "So?"

"She says he's been creeping her for weeks."

I look at Cali. "You beat him?"

She nods.

"He just wants a rematch."

Melanie shakes her head. "There's more. Show him."

Cali shakes her head and keeps her eyes glued to the screen.

I look closer and realize that her Saki's not the one winning. In fact, she's whiffing moves that I know she can connect.

Melanie passes me Cali's phone but I don't look at it. "She doesn't want me to."

"C'mon, Cali," Melanie says. "You should show your dad too."

Saki's win quote appears on the screen:

IT'S EXTRA COLD WHEN YOU'RE ALL ALONE!

CHAPTER 12

Cali puts her head under the pillow. "Whatever. It's so embarrassing," she mumbles.

I turn on the phone. She's got pictures of earlier comments from this guy and others. They call her things that would totally get someone suspended from school. But that's normal online. Melanie just doesn't get it.

"Those are the creepiest ones," Cali says, peeking out from the pillow. "What do you think I should do?"

"Nothing. That's just how gamers talk," I say.

"You say things like that?" Melanie asks.

I feel Kaigo's fire heat my cheeks. "Well, not that bad. Some of those messages are extra. But I hear stuff like that all the time."

"Did you see the last one?"

I flick through more screenshots. ShoMe goes on about wanting to play her. Says she sounds pretty. Then:

ShoMe   Tuesday , 7:36 pm
UR IN MTRL

Mel is reading over my shoulder. "C'mon, you have to admit that's messed up."

"How does he know where I am?" Cali asks. That wobble is back in her voice.

Is this what she meant by trouble? She's totally overreacting. Okay, maybe this guy is taking it a bit far, but still.

"He doesn't know exactly where you live. He probably just looked up your IP address and knows what city you're in. Don't let him freak you out. He's just trying to mess with you so he can have an advantage when you play again. It's normal."

"I don't know what's *normal* to you weirdos, but if someone sent me that, I'd be calling the cops. This ShoMe guy is stalking her. Cali, scroll up. Show him what the guy wrote today."

Cali's hand trembles as she uses the controller to scroll through her messages.

ShoMe   Friday, 10:00 pm
I'M IN MTRL TOO

She looks at me, like I should see what she means now.

I shake my head. "Don't worry. It's just mind games."

"Whatever." She closes the messages and starts a new match. The baby has finally stopped crying and it's quiet, except for Melanie's ranting, but I'm used to tuning her out. I'm so tired. I put my head down. The glow from the screen reflects off the green stone in the ring hanging from a chain around Cali's neck. Above it, Cali's face is lit up, while her black hair blends into the darkness. She looks like a fairy. I close my eyes.

When I open them, there's light coming through Cali's window. Melanie and Cali are asleep, head to feet, on the mattress on the floor. We need to leave in fifteen minutes!

◄o►

Me and Cali rush to get ready.

After my shower I have no choice but to throw on my clothes from yesterday and hope I don't stink too bad. I wonder if Yuudai Sato ever lost his luggage before a tournament. He'd probably still win, even with a gamepad, playing with one hand. That guy is godlike.

When we finally get Melanie up, she takes forever in the bathroom. We'll never make it on time.

Cali and I sit at the kitchen table with our shoes on. I've got the info package with the forms my mom signed under Cali's gamepad and I'm fidgeting with the controls.

Her dad is eating toast and reading on his phone. "When do you guys want to leave?" he asks.

Now!

"As soon as Melanie's ready," Cali answers.

Or we can just leave without her.

Marnie walks into the kitchen looking like a zombie. She makes coffee with her eyes half open and the baby on her hip. Then she puts Ruby in a baby seat on the table—the only place there's room for her—and flicks a button. The thing starts vibrating. The sound competes with my tapping thumbs.

Melanie finally comes out, stinking like a rose garden. She says good morning to everyone, and coochie coo to Ruby. Then she looks at me. "Make sure you bring two of those controllers."

"Ha, ha. I'm not going to lose another one."

"Didn't she tell you?" Melanie says. "Cali signed up last night."

"You're competing?"

"Don't be so rude," Melanie says.

"What? It's just a question."

"Listen to yourself," Melanie lectures. "Plus, that look on your face—so insulting."

It is? I try to make my face look normal. "Why'd you change your mind?"

"Because I *do* want to compete. I just never thought I could until Melanie said that stuff last night."

What's weird is that I never thought of it either. To be honest, I never thought of competing at a tournament myself until I got invited to T3. Maybe Cali just needed a push like that. Why didn't I ever think to ask her to sign up?

"And Melanie's right: I should stop letting people hold me back."

By people, does she mean me?

CHAPTER 13

The ride to the hotel feels like forever. The three of us are in the back of Mr. Chen's car, Cali in the middle.

I spend the ride freaking out over what to say to Kyle about my controller. Obviously I can't tell him the truth. He'd cut me from the team for sure if he found out I was so irresponsible.

I can't tell him it broke, because he'll want to see it and try to fix it.

I could tell him someone stole it. That wouldn't be my fault. Who knows, maybe someone *did* steal it. I mean, I never got a chance to check. Someone could even have picked up my case by mistake. There were a lot of small black suitcases on that shelf. It would be an honest mistake. By the end of the fifteen-minute drive, I've convinced myself that someone took my case by accident. Once they realize their mistake, they'll use our address on the tag to return it. I hope I'm still this confident when I talk to Kyle.

I'm super late for the meeting. Stupid Melanie. I throw my forms at her and tell her to go hand them in. She goes with Cali and her dad to the registration table. He needs to sign forms since Cali's twelve, like me.

The hotel restaurant is called Chez Antoine. It's long and narrow with tables along a wall of windows and booths on the other side. There are blue-checked cloths on all the tables. I find Kyle and four other guys at a table near the entrance. They've got plates in front of them with half-eaten eggs and sausages. All five are wearing red ArcadeStix T-shirts where the X is made out of two sticks of wood.

"Hey, JStar!" Kyle stands and shakes my hand. I've only seen him in person once before, at the T3 tournament when he asked me to join the ArcadeStix team. He's cut his hair in an army style and looks like a shorter version of that actor from the latest Spiderman movie.

"Everyone, meet our young prodigy, Jaden." Kyle goes around the table making introductions. "That's

Chris Chung," he says, pointing to a chubby guy with short spiky hair.

The guy looks up and nods, but doesn't smile.

That must be Chung-Key. I wonder if I should apologize for dropping off the other day after I invited him to play. But he's already focused back on his plate.

"Jeffy and Nicco are at the window there." He points to a couple of guys who are more interested in something on the one guy's phone than me. "They're playing *Mega Haunt* with me, so you won't compete against them."

"And this guy—who dyed his hair the wrong freaking color—is Sage." Kyle bops the electric-blue hair of the guy sitting next to him.

"C'mon. The blue complements the red shirt, don't you think, kid?"

The word *kid* makes me remember how much older all these guys are. They're probably all in college already. "Uh . . . totally," I say.

"Sit down and shut up," Kyle says. I sit down fast. He smiles and tosses me a red T-shirt. Yes! A clean shirt. "You're part of the ArcadeStix team now."

I feel like the Padawan to his Obi-Wan. "Yes, sir."

"I like this kid already," Sage says. "Did you hear that? Sir!"

A waiter comes by and asks if I want anything.

"Bring him the same as the rest of us," Kyle says. "But you're going to have to scarf it down fast. Only half an hour till game time."

Kyle pushes over the schedule and a competitor's pass attached to a neon-green lanyard. Then he pulls out some papers. "We were about to go over the matchups. Unfortunately, you're not going to have an easy path. This tournament is bigger than T3. It draws a lot of American players up for the weekend. They run the first day as a round-robin. In order to compete tomorrow, you need to prove yourself by making top two in your pool."

I read that in the package. There are eight pools of eight. You play everyone in your pool, and only the top two in each pool, sixteen players in total, come back to play for the prize on Sunday.

"Your pool has two players from our rival team. That's them over there." He points to a table of guys in neon-blue shirts with a picture of a power drink inside a big circle on the front. Now I get why the blue hair was a bad choice.

"They're going to do a lot of trash-talking," Sage says. "Don't let it get to you."

"Okay," I say.

"The good thing is you won't understand most of it." Sage laughs. "They're Frenchies."

Kyle continues. "Jaden, you have an easy match first. SaltyPeppa."

Sage dismisses this news with a *pfff* and a wave of his hand. "No problem. Just try to focus on the screen, not her legs."

"Rude," Chung-Key says.

"C'mon, why does she wear skirts that short if she doesn't want us to look?" Sage says.

"All right, that's enough. Let's keep this PG," Kyle says. "Sage and Chris, your pools each have an O in them too."

"What does that mean?" I ask.

"The power drink that sponsors the blue team is called O. Like *eau*, the French word for water," Kyle explains.

"Or *oooh!* like people scream when they watch us ooooown them," Sage adds.

I notice Melanie and Cali settling into a booth nearby. I wonder what pool she's in.

Chung-Key leans over. "You need to make top two. Don't make us look stupid for having a kid on our team."

There's that word again. *Kid.*

Kyle must see the panic in my eyes. "Don't worry about Jaden representing," he says. "He's solid. Since he started using our controller, he's been on the rise."

Crap! My thumbs drum the table. "Um, about that . . ."

Just then, a blue-shirt guy with long, wavy hair comes over and starts talking to us. "So, who is your new guy—JStar?" Sage wasn't kidding; the guy's French accent is so thick, the word *who* sounds like *ooh*. But worse, he pronounces the letter *J* in French and it almost sounds like the word *she*. That makes me *She-Star*.

Sage cracks up. "She-Star," he says with major exaggeration. "That's what I'm calling you now!"

"You mean JStar?" Kyle asks.

"You are *She-Star*?" the French guy asks Kyle.

"No, *she* is She-Star." Sage points to me. He's shaking with high-pitched screechy laughter. If anyone's a girl, it's him.

"Ah, you are *She-Star*?" The long-haired guy doesn't get the joke, or he doesn't care. He could pass for a girl himself with those long curls. My thumbs are tapping and I'm starting to sweat.

The French guy calls to his friends at the other table and holds his hand to his waist. "*Eh, le p'tit gars c'est She-Star.*"

I need to stop him from saying that stupid name again. "Who are you?" I ask.

"Me, I'm ORevoir," he says as he flicks his hair over his shoulder. "I am the winner of this tournament."

CHAPTER 14

"He's fronting," Sage says when ORevoir walks away. "Last tournament he drowned in the pools."

My food arrives and I look over at Cali. The guys have joined them now. Roy is sitting next to Melanie while Devesh and Hugh are squished into the other side of the booth with Cali. I'm sure it's no accident that Devesh is in the middle.

"Kyle," I say hesitantly. "There's something I need to tell you."

"Eat first," he says. "You need your energy. Game on in twenty minutes." He calls the waiter over and pays the bill on the spot. Then he and the other guys stand.

"Eat up. Then put on your shirt. We'll see you inside." I'm too nervous to eat much, so after a few bites I throw on the T-shirt and head over to my friends' table. Cali's got a competitor's pass around her neck now too.

Roy is reading her paper and laughing. "Who comes up with these names? PandaCandy? MrWinDoh? Actually, I like that one."

Melanie rolls her eyes. "Lame."

"Oh yeah? What would your tag be?" I ask. "Shopaholic?"

"Better than JStar." She switches to a singsong voice. "I'm so cool, I'm a star."

"That's nothing," Hugh says. "Devesh calls himself GodofGods. And he's not even a good player."

"Whatever, Catchup. Devesh *means* God of Gods, so it's legit."

Hugh points to his plate, which is a sea of red goop. "And I eat ketchup on everything, so mine's legit too!"

"I think I'd go with something like Ouch," says Roy.

"And that's why you don't play fighting games," I say. "We'd better go. Ready?"

"I guess," Cali says.

"She was born ready!" Devesh says.

Hugh and Devesh get up to let Cali out. "This is so cool! Both of you are competing!" His smile practically stretches off his face. Then it droops. "Wait. How are we going to watch you both?"

"I'm at station sixteen," I say.

"Twelve," Cali says.

"That's not too far apart," Devesh says. "We'll figure something out."

Hugh sits back down and picks up his fork. "I'll *catch up*," he says. "Get it?"

We all groan.

Cali follows me out of the restaurant with Devesh on her heels.

The banquet room where the tournament is being held is huge. Like T3, there are numbered stations along the walls, each one with two chairs facing a monitor. Some stations have crowds gathered, and when big moves happen, the spectators react loudly. In the middle of the room, chairs are set up in rows, half facing left and half facing right, so people can watch the two big screens at either end where matches are being streamed.

There's this cool energy in the room that's not just about all the gaming systems running in here. It's powered by excitement and nerves. It's like we're at a rock festival and me and Kaigo are about to perform. I remember the rush of playing on the big screen at T3. It felt amazing to have all those people behind me, cheering me on. There's nothing like the hype of tournament play!

We make our way through the crowd, following the station numbers from one up. We get to Cali's station first. I open my backpack and pass her a controller. She must be nervous, because she's not talking. I want to say something to encourage her. That's what a boyfriend would do. But I can't get a word past Devesh, who's rambling about how great she's going to do. Finally I just say "Good luck" and walk away.

Devesh doesn't make a move to follow me. So that's how it's going to be.

When I get to station sixteen I take out Cali's other gamepad and plug in. Then I sit tapping the buttons until SaltyPeppa shows up.

She's wearing a tight red miniskirt that gets even shorter when she sits down. She looks like Cali, but about ten years older—except for the clothes. I can't imagine Cali ever wearing a skirt like that. Cali's clothes look a lot like mine.

SaltyPeppa has an amazing controller. It's from ArcadeStix, too; it's shiny and gold but smaller than the one I lost. I'm trying to figure out what model it is when I realize it probably looks like I'm staring at her legs. Kaigo's fire shoots into my cheeks when she shakes my hand. I try to keep my eyes up. I don't even care about her legs, but after what Sage said, I can't stop thinking about not looking at them.

She selects Wendo, the kraken-cross. I'm glad to have the screen to focus on.

The *FIGHT!* sign flashes. I go on the attack by throwing my bread-and-butter combo: two crouching light punches followed by Dragon Claw. But it's like I have Saki's Yeti hands on the tiny controller, and I miss the button on the last move. Kaigo just jumps up and spins around.

SaltyPeppa may not be the best player, but she totally capitalizes on my miss. I don't play against the kraken-cross a lot. Wendo's hard to fend off because he grows eight tentacles when he performs his Super moves. All those arms are beating me to a pulp right now.

K.O.

This cannot happen. If I lose to a girl in the first round I'll be She-Star forever. I bet Yuudai Sato never lost a round to a girl. I've got to turn this around. Man, I miss my ArcadeStix controller. How could I have been so stupid to leave it on the train?

I press Start to begin round two.

"Jaden, what the hell, bro?" It's Kyle's voice from behind me, but I can't turn to look at him. I have to keep my eyes on the screen.

"Where's the controller we gave you?"

I hope I can get my story straight while I'm in the middle of a battle. "Tried to tell you. It's gone."

"Gone?"

"Someone took it. On the train."

"You can't play with that thing."

He's right. I'm getting killed. I crouch to block a jet of water. Too late—I'm blown to the edge of the screen.

Kyle mumbles something and leaves.

I want to hit Pause and see where he went, but the rules say pausing means you forfeit the round. So I continue getting beat up by SaltyPeppa. Arms are all around me. It's like being beaten by a mob instead of just one character.

K.O.

I've lost two rounds in a row. That means the first game is hers. If I lose another game I'll lose this match, along with my dignity.

CHAPTER 15

I look around. Where did Kyle go? What did he say? Did he kick me off the team? I'm seriously freaking when I see him running across the room with my ArcadeStix controller in his hands.

"Hold up," he says when he gets back. "Jaden's going to swap controllers."

"How'd you get my controller back?" For a second I wonder if the old lady from the train is here.

"It's one of the demos I brought along for people to try out."

"That's not allowed," SaltyPeppa says. "'Each competitor must provide their own controller.'" She's quoting from the rules.

"This *is* his controller," Kyle says. "He's on our team."

"You can't change in the middle of a match."

"Actually, you can if it's between games," I say

with confidence. But I don't want to be a jerk about it, so I press Start as soon as Kyle plugs in the ArcadeStix controller.

This is more like it. My hands don't feel so huge anymore. I just hope it's not too late.

I go straight to my bread-and-butter. This time Kaigo doesn't even move. What is happening? I follow the cord with my eyes to check that Kyle plugged it in right. He did.

Wendo juggles me from one tentacle to another at supersonic speed.

Kyle calls out, "Flip the switch!"

What's he talking about?

"I was using that controller for *Mega Haunt*. It's not on the right mode. Flip the switch next to the power button."

I follow his instructions, but it's too late for this round. Wendo is body-slamming me hard and my health is almost gone.

When the *FIGHT!* sign flashes again, I'm back. No more misses. Now Wendo hits the ground, fast and hard. When my Super Meter is full, I combo into Dragon Breath Super and fry Wendo up. Calamari, anyone?

Kyle pats my back. "That's more like it!"

I take four rounds in a row to win the match. Should have won them all, but I'll take it.

I shake hands with SaltyPeppa, making sure to look her in the eyes.

Then I head back to station twelve where Devesh and Hugh are watching Cali. The guy she's playing is older. He's got a beard and a belly, and looks kind of like Mr. E. Guys like this, who've been playing forever, are called OG, like Original Generation. I hear they prefer Original Gangstas, which is kind of funny. These guys sure don't look like thugs.

"How's she doing?" I ask Hugh.

"Game three, round three."

In other words, whoever wins this round takes the match.

On screen, Cali's Saki is locked in battle with Lerus, the unicorn-cross. Their Health Meters are about equal.

Saki tosses Lerus through the air, spins to become a Yeti, and breathes snow all over his opponent. The OG's Health Meter goes down, but it's not enough.

Lerus spins into a unicorn and gallops at Saki with her horn down. Cali reacts fast and jumps

Saki out of the way. But Lerus kicks her from behind. Now it's Cali's Health Meter that's dropping.

Back in human form, Lerus and Saki box it out. It won't take much at this point. Both have only tiny slivers of health left.

"C'mon, Cali, you can do this!" Devesh says.

And he's right. A jab to the head and Lerus is K.O.

"Yeah!" The three of us scream in unison.

Cali gets up and shakes hands with her opponent. She's blushing.

Hugh and Devesh give her high fives. "You were amazing!" Devesh says. I'm surprised he doesn't try to hug her, like yesterday.

She smiles.

From what I could see she almost lost. But I don't want to look like a jerk after everyone's congratulated her. "Way to keep calm under pressure," I say.

"Thanks," she says, looking down.

It's Hugh who finally notices what I'm carrying. "Dude, how'd you get your controller back?"

I tell them what happened. Well, most of it. I don't mention that I was losing at first. Hey, it was their choice to watch Cali instead of me.

Sage walks by and spots me. "Hey, She-Star. Your pal ORevoir is playing Chris on stream. Come support the team."

We follow him. Chung-Key and ORevoir are setting up on the stage. The organizers select people to play up there when they expect a good fight. These matches show up on the big screen for everyone at the tournament to see, but they're also streamed live for anyone watching at home. I wonder if Ty and Flash will watch to see if we really went to Montreal. Or Hailey. I imagine her mesmerizing eyes watching the live-stream and my thumbs start to tap.

It's still early, and the pool matches don't usually draw huge crowds, but seats are filling up. There's a hot tension in the room, like the energy from all these gaming consoles is vibrating toward the stage.

We can't find five seats together close up, so me and Kyle sit in the third row and my friends sit in the three seats in front of us. I keep my backpack with the controller in it on my lap so there's no chance I can forget it again.

"So, this is your posse," Sage says.

"Oh, yeah. This is Cali, Hugh, and Devesh."

"You guys playing or watching?"

"She's playing." Devesh points to Cali.

"Nice! How you doing so far?"

"I'm doing okay—"

"She's killing it!" Devesh breaks in. "She's goddesslike!"

"You teach her to play?" Sage asks me.

"Sort of." I mean, we play together a lot.

"Nice," Sage says. Cali rolls her eyes and turns back to face the stage.

"She even beat Jaden," Devesh says. Again.

"Oh yeah?" Sage raises his eyebrows.

I glare at Devesh. "Once."

"It's cool when a girl can keep up with the guys," Sage says. Then, quietly, he adds, "And it's hot. She your girlfriend?"

I shrug.

"Yeah, she is. Look at you turning red."

Why does everyone keep saying that? Maybe she is. I'm glad the match is starting so we can talk about something else.

Sage says, "We'd better hope Chris wins. He's no fun when he loses."

So that was Chung-Key being fun at breakfast?

I'm not surprised that ORevoir plays Goyle, the griffin-cross. A griffin has the head and claws of an eagle and the body of a lion. This character is super aggressive and totally arrogant. I hate playing Goyle because he's one of the only characters in the game that can fill his Super Meter by performing taunts.

Chung-Key plays Blaze, the phoenix-cross. He teleports behind ORevoir and kicks him in the back with a seven-hit combo. Then he spins through the air and spits fire from above. We yell for every Super like we're at a rock concert, but it's nothing compared to the noise of the home crowd cheering for ORevoir.

ORevoir uses every opportunity to play his taunt. Instead of attacking, he stands with open arms, basically saying, "Come on, hit me with your best

shot." The disrespect fuels the fires of rivalry and the home crowd goes crazy.

And he's not just taunting in the game. After each round, ORevoir leans over and says stuff to Chung-Key. Chung-Key never responds; his shoulders just inch up closer to his ears. On screen, he whiffs a grab here, back dashes, there. He's getting mad and making mistakes.

ORevoir jumps up and spins like a corkscrew into Chung-Key, then follows with a twelve-kick combo to the head. Chung-Key rallies with a ten-hit combo of uppercuts, but it's not enough.

The taunts, the crowd, and Chung-Key's own frustration are just too much. ORevoir takes the match.

"Uh-oh. He's gonna be salty!" Sage says. "Stay away from him for a bit."

I was planning to avoid him anyways.

Sage gives me a fist bump before we hustle to our next matches. As he leaves he winks at Cali. "I'll keep my eye on you, pretty lady."

Cali gives a sarcastic smile. Why's she being so rude?

CHAPTER 16

I claim an easy win against a noob next, but it's my third matchup that gives me the shakes. I'm playing a guy from the O team. I look around as I sit down. Still no sign of Hugh or Devesh. I could really use some support here.

The guy's tag is OMG. That's probably what people say when they see him. He's tall and wide and scary looking. The funny thing is he chooses Ylva, a skinny girl wearing a cavewoman dress.

She looks easy to beat, but she's the matchup I struggle with the most. She's the dire wolf–cross —she's fast and tricky. Thank god Kyle got me this controller. I'd have no chance without it.

The first two rounds go by fast. OMG keeps close and sinks Ylva's canine teeth into my neck before I can get blocks up.

In the second game I keep my distance by sticking to Dragon Tail Supers, since I can swipe from farther away. On screen the girl goes flying every time my tail takes her out. We're tied at a game each.

I take the first round in game three. Then that idiot ORevoir shows up to cheer on his teammate. Or, more accurately, to trash-talk me. He stands right behind me.

"Ha, miss," he calls when I whiff an uppercut.

When my Dragon Tail Super is blocked, he yells, "You suck!" Real creative.

I could really use my friends right now, but they're all watching Cali play. Again.

OMG takes the second round in game three. It's all down to this last round.

I don't let OMG trick me into getting too close. When my Super Meter is full I back dash. ORevoir calls, "Yeah, run away, baby." He doesn't know my plan. I act like I'm retreating, and from the very corner of the screen I throw Dragon Fire Super. Kaigo transforms into a dragon and swirls across the screen in a gray smoke tornado.

K.O.

ORevoir doesn't have anything to say now.

◄○►

Cali won her next match too, and the one after that.

"You should have seen her, J. She's on fire," Devesh gushes when we meet up again.

"Well, she played Saki, so technically she's on ice . . . ," Hugh says. We're sitting on some lounge chairs in the hallway outside the banquet hall, chilling before our next matches. I'm hugging my backpack with the controller in it. Every time one of the double doors opens the energy and noise from the room spills out to us.

"Great!" I don't mention how close I just came to losing.

Cali's fiddling with her gamepad. She doesn't even look my way. Is she freezing me out? What's her problem?

"Is that guy who was bugging you here?" I say, partly because I'm curious and partly because I'm annoyed with her.

She throws me a cold stare.

"What guy?" Devesh asks.

Ugh, now he's going to go all *poor Cali, I'll take care of you.*

"It's nothing. Right, Jaden? You said it's not a big deal." Her eyes are as icy as Saki's.

"What are you talking about?" Hugh asks.

Now I have to tell them, because she's not going to. "There's this guy who's been trolling her online and trying to get her to rematch."

If she could, Cali would throw ice daggers at me right now.

"Is he here?" Devesh asks.

When we all stare at her long enough she finally answers. "Yeah. I saw him listed in another pool."

"We'll stay with you, just in case," Devesh says.

"I can take care of myself," Cali says, and she storms off.

"What's wrong with her?" Hugh asks.

"Girls," Devesh says.

"Shut up, Devesh," I say. I don't even know who I'm mad at now. All I know is that things were a lot easier before everyone started pointing out that Cali is a girl. I wish we could go back to when she was just Cali.

Melanie rushes in from the main lobby. Her and Roy have been missing in action since breakfast. She's out of breath, like she's been running to find me. I think she's coming to yell at me about Cali, but instead, she pushes her phone in my face. "It's Mom."

"Again?" I bet Yuudai Sato's mom doesn't call him when he's at tournaments. I put the phone to my ear. "*Wei?*"

"*Er zi*, how are you?"

"I'm fine, *Ma ma*." We already talked twice last night and once this morning. "Didn't *jie jie* tell you I'm fine?"

"Yes. I'm just worried. How is Cali?"

"She's great," I lie. "She's playing in the tournament too."

"What? Be careful she doesn't beat you again."

OMG. Is there anyone on this planet who doesn't know? "Funny, *Ma ma*. I have to go. Here's *jie jie*."

Melanie waves me off.

I cover the phone and whisper. "You want me to tell her who else is here?"

She grabs the phone out of my hand and stomps away.

I turn back to my friends. "So, Roy's staying with you guys?"

"Yeah. I told my uncle I was coming with two friends anyway, so he's your replacement. Roy's cool. Did you know he meditates?"

"What?"

"Yeah, last night he taught us. We all stared at a candle and tried to think about nothing but the flame."

"Think of nothing?" I chuckle. "That's easy for you guys."

"Sounds easy, but it's not." Hugh is super serious. "Then, after, I slept so good. You should try it."

"I don't think it will work with a baby crying all night long," I say.

"And this morning he made us do this gratitude thing where we can't get up until we spend two minutes thinking about someone we're grateful for," Hugh says.

"Are you serious? Who'd you think about?" I ask.

"My dad."

Devesh jumps in. "And I'm pretty sure Roy was thinking about your sister."

"Eww, gross! Shut up!"

I don't ask who Devesh thought about.

◄o►

It's like Devesh and Hugh disappear whenever I have a match. Even after Cali told us off, they still watch her matches instead of mine. I look around for them before I start and after, but during battles I have to keep my focus. I win my fourth match easily, even without any support. I worry when my fifth match is against the other O team player, OhOh, but it turns out I don't need to. The guy keeps yawning and makes some really stupid mistakes.

I don't know how anyone could be yawning here. The room has so much hype—this power that flows from station to station and game to game, and it's keeping me fueled. Even though I hardly slept last night, I'm so wired from all the energy flowing around me that I'm the most awake I've ever been. Now that I've got my controller back and put those two Os behind me, I'm invincible!

And hungry.

I pack the controller in my backpack, strap it on, and look around again for Devesh and Hugh. I find them wandering in the lobby. I don't ask how Cali did.

Hugh tells me anyways. "You should have seen it, J. She won big time against this girl. She was like, 'Take that, sister,' and Saki went all Yeti-Yeti-bang-bang on Wendo."

"I think she's actually the best girl player here," Devesh says.

"She is." Hugh pulls out a piece of paper where he's been scribbling the results of matches. "She's the only undefeated girl so far."

"She's undefeated?"

"Just like you!" Hugh says.

"You nervous about playing her?" Devesh asks.

That will only happen if she makes Top 16. Is that even possible? Maybe—she's in an easy pool. I don't have time to think about it anymore, because Mel comes out of nowhere, grabs my hand, and pulls. "Come. I found the guy. He's playing at station seven."

"What guy?" Hugh asks.

But I already know who she's talking about.

CHAPTER 17

When we get to station seven, I see a skinny Filipino man who is older than my dad. "Oh, gross." I'm starting to get why Melanie is so freaked out.

"Not him," Melanie says. "The other guy, with the blue hair."

I laugh. "Try again, Nancy Drew. That's Sage. He's on my team."

"His gamertag is ShoMe, exactly like the guy who sent all those messages."

This is too weird. "But that guy said he's from Montreal."

"Not exactly. He said he's in Montreal now, probably for this tournament." Melanie is losing it. "Imagine how weird it is for her to be here with this guy, after all those creepy things he wrote."

I think back to when we were all watching Chung-Key play ORevoir. What did Sage say to Cali?

I'll keep my eye on you, pretty lady. Is that creepy? Does he know she's the person he's been messaging?

Roy and Cali come and join us from where they were standing, off to the side. She does look freaked out, probably because Melanie is putting crazy ideas into her head. "You've got it wrong, Mel. He's a nice guy." And a good player. He's decimating his opponent. When the match ends, Sage shakes the guy's hand and comes over to us.

"How's it going, She-Star?" He clasps my hand and pulls me in for a bro hug. "Any losses yet?"

"Nah. You?" I ask. Maybe if I show them that he's a normal guy, Melanie will stop freaking the freak out.

"Only wins for me." He turns to Cali. "And you're still undefeated? Nice! Can't wait to play you next round." She doesn't meet his eyes or answer. Has he been watching her? How does he know she's undefeated?

"Don't worry, I won't bite. Anyways, I know you already have a boyfriend, right, She-Star?"

I don't know what to say so I just smile awkwardly.

"Let's go to the hotel restaurant," Sage says. "Business lunch. I'll give you guys the scoop on some of your next competitors."

Roy jumps in. "No thanks. We're going to Mr. Burger down the street."

"They've got burgers at Chez Antoine," Sage says.

Melanie gives Sage a dirty look. "We have plans." She takes my hand and Cali's, like we're little kids.

I pull my hand back. Melanie and Cali walk away with Devesh following, as usual.

"You coming?" Roy asks.

"Free burgers?" Hugh gives a nervous chuckle. "Of course we're coming, right J?"

I know they all want me to come so that Melanie and Cali don't get mad. But Sage has been to a bunch of tournaments and he's willing to help me out. This is a major opportunity. He could give me advice that

will make the difference between winning and losing. Maybe he says some stupid things to girls, but
he's only ever been nice to me. "Nah, you guys go
ahead. I'm gonna eat with Sage."

◄○►

"Tournament play is not like playing at home," Sage
explains while we're waiting for our burgers. "You
need to adapt to your opponent's style."

I try to concentrate on what he's saying, but
Melanie's got me so angry. It's all her fault that Cali's
mad at me now. Melanie's got her all freaked out
over nothing. She doesn't even know Sage. I can't
believe she said Cali should call the police. That's
stupid. He's a good guy. Here he is taking the time
to help me out.

"For example, you're playing MrWinDoh next.
He's hard to beat. He's a turtle. Stays on the defen-
sive and tries to take as little damage as possible.
Just waits for you to make a mistake so he can strike.
You need to play defensive too or you'll be an easy
target."

I don't care what Melanie thinks. She's an idiot.
What *is* bugging me is the fact that Roy is taking
her side. I can usually count on Roy. Why was he

trying to get me to stay away from Sage? I mean, there was that comment about SaltyPeppa's legs this morning. But that was just a compliment. He was saying she's pretty, right? But what about when he said that Cali was hot? Was that a compliment too? Sage is eighteen, like Roy. Does that make it creepy? Roy's probably just taking Melanie's side because she's his girlfriend and he has to do what she says. The more I think about it, the more I think having a girlfriend is overrated.

Sage is still talking. "Now the O team, they mostly rely on rushdown. To survive, you need to stay calm. Don't panic and button mash like they want you to. Stand your ground and frustrate them by blocking."

I hope I remember some of this when I need it.

I wonder what Josh would think of Sage. Josh and Melanie are twins, but they don't agree on anything. Would he like Sage? He's lucky there are no girls on his sports teams to complicate things.

We spy Chung-Key and Kyle at the entrance to the restaurant. Sage waves them over.

Kyle's all smiles as usual, and Chung-Key is his opposite. I didn't know eyes could frown, but his perma-frown now has two matching mini-frowns above it.

Sage puts his arm on Chung-Key's shoulder. "Chris, man, let it go. You're stressing everyone out."

Chung-Key swipes the arm away.

"Ignore him," Kyle tells us. "It's only one match. He'll still make it through."

"I was giving She-Star the lowdown on some opponents," Sage says.

Chung-Key looks up. I swear even his nose is frowning. "You'd better not teach him how to beat me."

◄o►

When I get to my station, there's no sign of Hugh and Devesh. Instead, the same OG Cali played in her first match is sitting there. Must be a mistake. "I'm looking for MrWinDoh."

"That's me," he replies. "Waiting for JStar. That you?"

"Yeah. It's just . . . I'm confused. You played my friend in the first match, a girl my age. But she's in a different pool."

"Imperio?"

"No, HermIone. Or VoldemorT?"

"My first game was against a young girl, all right. She beat my a— um . . . butt too. But her tag was Imperio."

What the . . . ? Imperio is my next and last game. That's Cali? She's using *another* tag?

The guy mumbles as he selects his character, Cantu. "Didn't drive all the way up here from Boston to get kicked out by kids. If I lose this one, I'm gonna retire from this sport."

All through our match, I'm doing mental back dashes. Cali was in my pool this whole time? But she keeps winning. And Kyle even said this was not an easy pool.

Fortunately, I remember some of what Sage told me about this guy. He really is a turtle! All defense, only ever attacking when he has a sure hit. I play a highly defensive game and pull off a victory; my usual tactics would have left me exposed.

I can't believe Cali beat this guy in her first-ever tournament game.

"I hope you don't retire, sir," I say as we shake hands. "You're a beast."

As I walk away, Devesh and Hugh rush up to me. I haven't seen them since before lunch and I'm kind of pissed. They're supposed to be my friends, but they've been watching all of Cali's matches instead of mine. They're totally taking her side in this.

"Why didn't you guys tell me Cali is Imperio?" My Kaigo side roars at them.

"You didn't know?" Hugh asks.

"No. She always uses *Harry Potter* names."

"It *is* from *Harry Potter*. Remember the Imperio curse?" Hugh says with a dopey smile. "The one for mind control?"

Makes sense. She's been playing mind games with me all day.

"Listen, man, I've got an idea." Devesh looks around, then whispers, "You should throw this match."

CHAPTER 18

"You're messed up." I start to walk away, but Hugh calls me back.

"Dude, hear him out."

"Think about it," Devesh says. "What happens if you lose this match?"

"Um, I lose my perfect record for the day."

"Okay, but you still move on, right?" Hugh says.

"Depends if the O guys lost to anyone else besides me."

Hugh whips out his paper. "OhOh lost to Cali and OMG, so he's out."

What? Cali beat an O? I know the guy was tired, but still. That's impressive.

"And OMG lost to MrWinDoh."

"Then I'll make Top 16 either way, but . . ."

"Exactly!" Devesh's monobrow is halfway up his

forehead. "But if Cali loses, she's out. She'd be tied with OMG, but he'll move on because he won their matchup."

Looks like Cali's not the only one playing mind games today. Now she's got Devesh helping her. "You want me to let her win? You are *so* desperate. Following her around all day, telling her she's amazing. You think she's going to fall in love with you if you rig the tournament for her?"

"Shut up, dude." Hugh's eyes are squinty-angry behind his glasses. "Are you trying to lose all your friends today?"

I freeze. What's going on? Hugh always agrees with me.

"Dude, we're trying to help you," Hugh says. "I told Devesh that Cali's your girlfriend."

"You what?" I say. "Why'd you say that?"

"Isn't she? You didn't deny it when I told Flash and Ty, so I just figured . . ."

"It's so obvious," Devesh says. "Anyways, we've been trying to look out for her since you're busy playing matches."

I'm so confused. Is Cali my girlfriend? I think back to everything that happened today. Maybe Devesh wasn't hitting on Cali. Was I just imagining it? Am I jealous? Is this what having a girlfriend is like?

Hugh says, "We can tell she's mad at you about something."

"So, if you let her win and make Top 16 with you, she can't be mad anymore," Devesh says.

"She'll see how much you care about her— enough to sacrifice. You'll be the hero."

I'm not sure about that last part, but the rest actually makes sense. "This was your idea?" I ask Devesh.

He nods.

"You know I'll get DQ'd if anyone finds out."

"No one will know. She beat you before, so it's not impossible."

He had to say it again. But, he's got a point. This plan could actually fix my problems with Cali. I should have known that my friends always have my back.

A guy in a yellow STAFF shirt carrying a clipboard comes up to us. "JStar? I need you to come with me."

Oh no! We stare at each other as we follow him. Is this place bugged? I can't believe I'm being DQ'd for fixing a match. What will Kyle say?

Then I realize he's leading me to the stage. Now I'm freaking out even more.

I want to throw the match for Cali. I want to be her hero. But it's one thing to lose in the corner with a small group watching. It's another deal entirely to lose on the big screen in front of everyone here, and all the people watching at home. To a girl.

Ty and Flash will never let me live this down. I wonder if Hailey is watching. My stomach flip kicks itself and I almost lose my lunch.

I might not even have to lose on purpose. It would be just like me to win six matches in a row, and then totally choke in front of an audience.

Cali's already on the stage, and she looks scared. It's her first time playing on the live-stream.

I want to start this off right. "Sorry," I say even though I'm not totally sure what I did. Then I stick my hand out. "Truce?"

She sighs and shakes my hand.

"Don't be nervous," I say. "Just pretend we're playing at home, like always."

"There's no crowd in my room," she says.

"Don't worry. I've got you," I say.

FIGHT!

I let her come on the attack and hit me with a flurry of punches before I back dash out of range. She comes at me with her Blizzard Super and I'm buried. I act like I didn't see her cross up coming and let her get in a Yeti headbutt from behind. Of course, I can't make it look too obvious, so whenever her lead gets big, I throw a Dragon Fire Super to even things out.

She wins the first two rounds to take game one.

"What are you doing?" she hisses.

"Um, losing to you again, I guess. You're on fire."

"I hate you, Jaden. I seriously can't stand you right now."

This isn't going how we planned. Why's she mad? Where's the thanks? We're supposed to be friends again, or whatever we are.

What do I do now?

The next round I'm all over the place. I throw my Dragon Fire Super, then back off a bit while she gets some good hits in.

"Don't you dare," she says while the crowd cheers.

A blizzard and I'm K.O.

She turns and glares at me. I've never seen her so pissed. "If you let up, even a little, I swear I will never speak to you again."

Now I'm mad too. I'm trying to do something nice for her, helping her get into the Top 16, even after she didn't talk to me all day, and she's mad at me for it?

Whatever. Game on!

CHAPTER 19

Being mad doesn't affect Cali's game. If anything she plays better. The good thing is I know her so well. I can take advantage of her weaknesses. Sometimes I can guess what she'll do before she even makes the move.

I jump up and breathe fire down her neck, but she blocks. Crap! That move used to get her every time. My advantage is also a disadvantage—she knows me just as well, and she saw that coming.

As soon as I can, I Super into Dragon Tail. It's the one I use the least, and I'm right to guess that she won't be expecting it. She blocks high, expecting Dragon Breath, but my tail swipes low and knocks her off her feet. Before she's out of hit-stun I add my go-to combo and watch her health drop.

The crowd cheers as I finish her off with a simple fireball.

In round three we poke at each other for a bit until she moves in to throw her favorite combo, which starts with snowballs. She always ends in a yeti headbutt, so I back away. But she sends a Flash Freeze my way instead. The millisecond I'm out of hit-stun she breathes icy air at me and freezes me solid.

Is it my imagination or is the crowd cheering louder for her than for me?

I've got my powerful Dragon Fire Super mastered, and I'm using it. No mercy.

K.O.

Now we're tied, one game each.

In game three my strategy is simple: play differently than I usually do so she can't guess my next move.

It's Cali's strategy too, but she takes it one step further. She changes characters for game three. Now she's playing Ylva, the dire wolf–cross she knows I struggle with.

It's actually really hard to change up my game play. I automatically use my bread-and-butter combo whenever I don't know what to do, and she automatically blocks it and sometimes even beats me to the punch.

She's got Ylva moving so fast. She must have been practicing her a lot. Her Wolf Tail Super takes me to the edge, then my Dragon Tail Super sends her flying. We lock arms and she wins, throwing me over her shoulder.

Now I'm K.O.

By round two we're both on pure attack, hardly bothering to block and defend. The crowd loves it. Every hit gets a noisy reaction and Supers make them scream, "Oh!"

I take round two when it times out. It's all down to the last round.

"You can do this, Cali," I hear Devesh in the crowd. "You beat him before!" I turn around and glare at him. His stupid plan got me here. If I had played full out from the start I would have beaten her by now.

Wouldn't I?

Devesh is gesturing angrily at me. He points to Cali and me and then to the door, like he's saying we could both make the next round. Hugh just makes a heart with his hands. I don't want Cali to make Top 16 anymore. And I definitely don't love her. I wish she'd never come to this tournament. I wish she never even started playing *Cross Ups*.

FIGHT!

I rip into her with jabs and kicks, but I'm so panicked I'm on autopilot. She's fast to defend because she knows all my best moves. I, on the other hand, can't figure out her strategy with Ylva. She's constantly jumping over me, like she's playing a kangaroo instead of a giant wolf. These cross ups are making me dizzy.

I shouldn't be surprised. Everything about Cali is a cross up lately. She's playing a different character in the game, but I feel like she's playing a different person in real life too.

One last wolf tail swipe and I'm K.O.

I rip my controller out of the console and stomp off the stage.

◄O►

Devesh and Hugh can't believe it either.

"So, did you let her win or did she beat you?" Devesh asks.

"I don't even know." All I know is I would have totally won the match if I hadn't given her the first game. Probably.

"I don't get girls," Hugh says.

"I don't even want to get girls," I say.

"The main thing is, you guys are both still in this, and you get to come back tomorrow and win this thing," Hugh says.

"Do you think she has a chance?" Devesh asks.

"Shut up. Obviously Jaden's going to win."

I wish I was as confident as Hugh.

◄O►

Devesh wasn't kidding. His uncle's place is huge. You could probably fit ten of Cali's dad's houses inside. All the furniture is white and looks tiny.

"It's called minimalist," Devesh explains.

Even the ceilings are super high. There must be way more air. So why do I feel like I can't catch a breath?

Since it was only three o'clock when we finished at the tournament, Devesh invited us all to hang out here. I don't think Cali likes the idea, but Melanie convinced her to come along because she can't bring Roy back to Cali's dad's place.

The room the guys are sharing is empty except for three mattresses on the floor and the guys' bags. It feels as big as Cali's dad's whole house.

Hugh kicks some socks under a mattress and we all plop onto the floor. I sit against one wall with Hugh and lean against my backpack with the controller in it. I'm keeping this thing close! Cali sits on the opposite side of the room. Even in this huge place, it feels like there's not enough space between us.

Devesh sits in the middle of the room, takes out the laptop he brought, and pulls up the streams from today.

"Show us the match where Cali beat Jaden," Melanie says. She must notice the tension in the room. My caring big sister has turned back into her dragon self.

Devesh acts like he can't find it. Melanie grabs the computer and looks herself.

"So, what happened, Jaden? You choke?" She's not interested enough to watch the actual match footage. But she's scrolling the comments. "Who wrote this?" she asks before reading out loud.

TygerFlash: @JSTAR is the biggest loser ever and he told us Cali is his girlfriend IRL.

Hugh and I lock eyes. "Ty and Flash!"

"You idiot!" I say. "Why'd you have to tell them about the tournament?"

"And why are they saying I'm Jaden's girlfriend?" Cali asks quietly.

Ha! I was right. I knew she wasn't.

"They kept teasing him about this girl Hailey at camp. So I said he already has a girlfriend, you know, to shut them up," Hugh rambles. "I mean, you are his friend and you're a girl, and . . ."

"Ugh, so embarrassing."

She thinks it's embarrassing to be my girlfriend? Okay, I know where I stand now. That's probably the same reaction Hailey would have.

"What the . . . " Melanie is scrolling through the comments. "Look at this." She points to a comment for Roy to read.

"I'm not reading that," he says.

CHAPTER 20

I don't want them reading any more stupid comments out to Cali. "Ty and Flash are idiots. Just ignore whatever they wrote."

"This isn't from your school friends. It's your teammate." Melanie reads:

ShoMe: New outfit & imperio will rule stream
ShoMe: Shorter + Tighter = Better

I look at Cali. She's wearing jeans and a black T-shirt, like always. "What?"

"Duh, he wants her to dress sexy." Melanie shakes her head in frustration.

I remember Sage's comments about SaltyPeppa's legs. "He just says stuff like that. He likes girls."

Melanie loses it. "I can't believe you're defending him. You just met him today. Look what he said about your best friend." She turns to Roy. "You should see the things he wrote to her online too."

"He doesn't even know that Cali is VoldemorT. He only knows her as Imperio from the tournament. Even I didn't know she changed her tag until right before we played. My *best friend* didn't tell me."

"Hold on. You think it's better if he thinks he's disrespecting two *different* female players?"

I wish Josh was here. My brother is on tons of sports teams. He'd tell them guys talk like that in the locker room too.

"It's just guy talk. Anyways, gamers are always saying rude stuff to throw their opponents off their game by getting them mad or frustrated. Last week one guy called me 'vomit's ugly brother,' and today ORevoir called me *tabarnak*, which I know means something pretty bad. I can only imagine the stuff he said to Chung-Key during their match."

"There's a difference between an insult and telling someone to wear less clothes."

"You're making a big deal out of nothing. That's just how guys talk. C'mon, Roy, tell her."

"Maybe that's the way gamers talk, but it's not cool, J."

Devesh jumps to my rescue. "That *is* how gamers talk. I get that stuff all the time in the comments when I stream a match with a girl player. They call girls eye candy, tell them to go back to the kitchen—"

"That's not trash talk," Roy says. "That's girl-bashing."

"Same thing," I say. Isn't it?

Roy is serious. "Think about it. Do they tell girls they 'play like a boy'? Do they tell you how to dress?"

"So? They say other things. They tell me I suck or I'm a try-hard," I say.

"Yeah, but you can practice and get better and change your playing style," he says. "Cali can't change that she's a girl."

"The guy's a jerk." Melanie bangs the laptop closed.

"That's my teammate you're talking about."

"Well, that's Cali he's talking about," Melanie says. "Would you say those things to her?"

Cali sighs and closes her eyes.

Hugh says, "They're not actually talking to each other."

"What'd you do now, Jaden?" Melanie says.

Even Melanie can't be angry at me for trying

to be a hero. "Get this. She's mad because I let her win so she could make Top 16. I thought she'd be happy . . ."

My words trail off when Roy looks up. His eyes are like laser beams that fix right onto mine.

"You *what*?" Melanie yells.

Roy shakes his head behind her back.

"I was trying to be nice . . ." Now Roy's making huge *X*s with his arms too.

"Oh my god. Jaden, you are so clueless. Why is Cali even friends with you?"

I look at Roy. "What did I do wrong?"

He sighs. "So many things, Jaden. So many things."

I give up. But Hugh doesn't. He jumps in to defend me. "Look, Cali, we know you're mad at Jaden. We thought it would help if he let you make Top 16."

"Let me?" Cali spits out the words.

"Not let you," I stammer. "Help you."

Roy cringes.

Cali stands up. "So what, I'm supposed to thank you now?"

I'm guessing the answer is no, but I can't figure out why.

"Thanks for the pity win." She walks out of the room.

Everyone waves me to follow her. But what am I supposed to say?

"Go!" Melanie says and pushes me out the bedroom door.

The house is so big and open that I can see Cali sitting on the narrow white living-room sofa from the upstairs hall railing. Everything is so white that it looks like she's sitting in Saki's snow cave. I head down the spiral staircase and sit next to her.

"Leave me alone."

This real-life stuff is way harder than any battle in *Cross Ups*. I wish there was some game feature I

could use to get past this. Maybe Kaigo could give Saki roses or something. Instead, all I can think of to say is "I'm sorry." Is that lame?

Cali stares at me. "How would you feel if you found out that the only reason you beat MrWinDoh today was because he let you win?"

Did he? Sometimes adults let kids win so they'll feel good about themselves. "That would suck," I say honestly.

"I know you were trying to be nice. But I want to win because I'm a good player, not because someone feels sorry for me."

"I just wanted you to stop being mad at me." She doesn't say anything. "It didn't work, and I don't know what to do next."

"Did you let me win last week too?"

"No," I say quickly. "I wish."

"You say the only way to earn respect as a gamer is in the game. But I beat you and you still don't respect me."

"I respect you."

"Then stop acting like I'm different from the guys."

"Okay," I say, even though I'm not sure what she means. She's not a guy.

The sound of clapping comes from upstairs. We look up. Everyone is standing at the railing, watching us. But they're not clapping. It's Melanie's phone. Her ringtone is a golf clap.

She grabs the phone out of her pocket and sighs. "Surprise. It's Mom again." She heads into the boys' room followed by Roy.

"So, are you Jaden's girlfriend again?" Hugh asks.

"What? Why do people keep saying that? Do you think I'm your girlfriend?"

"Not exactly. It's just, people keep saying you are . . ."

"Ugh! That's exactly what I'm talking about. Did anyone ask *me*? I'm not your girlfriend, and if you don't start treating me normal, like you treat Hugh and Devesh, I won't be your friend anymore either." She looks up at the railing. "That goes for you guys too. Stop following me around like I'm some princess who needs to be protected."

Hugh and Devesh head back to the guys' room mumbling apologies.

Cali leans back on the sofa. "Ugh! I wish it could be like old times when no one cared that you're a boy and I'm a girl."

That's what I said. But now that everyone made me think of Cali as a girl, and even a girlfriend, she seems different. I'm not sure if things can go back to the way they were.

CHAPTER 21

Cali's hanging with Roy and Melanie in the living room, listening to music. She probably doesn't want to be around me.

Me, Devesh, and Hugh chill in the guys' room.

"What do you think happened to your suitcase?" Hugh says.

"No idea. Lost and Found doesn't open till Monday."

"You left a suitcase with an electronic device inside on a national train car. I bet the bomb squad came and blew it up," Devesh says.

"They wouldn't blow it up," Hugh counters. "They'd use bomb-sniffing dogs to check it first."

"Even worse, I bet the dogs peed on your controller."

We watch playback from the tournament to see how the other Top 16 competitors play. Besides my teammates and Cali there's ORevoir, three more guys from his O team, and eight other top players. I don't feel confident against any of them, not even Cali.

When we get to my match against Cali I say, "We don't need to watch this one."

"We should totally watch," Devesh says. "When she played Ylva she owned you. You need to study that."

He's right. I need to be prepared in case I play her again. I click *PLAY*.

Even though Cali caught on fast that I was throwing the match, I must have been doing an okay acting job because the commentators don't mention anything.

"JStar really ramped up his play in game two, but the change to Ylva has thrown him off here in game three."

Was it that obvious?

It's amazing how fast *Cross Ups* seems when you're not in control. Even though I played that match, I have trouble following all the action.

"Look at that cross up and—oh! The juggle! She's really taking control of this match." The commentator's words sting.

"These are promising young players," the other commentator says. "Watching these up-and-comers gives me hope for the future of *Cross Ups*. Not a lot of kids put in the work to become stellar at 2-D fighting games anymore."

"I agree. The next generation is before our eyes. These two are closely matched. But I have to say, he relies too heavily on the crouching light punch–Dragon Claw combo, and she's figured it out."

The guy's right. I'd better change that up.

Cali knocks on the door just as she's finishing me off on screen.

"Devesh, your family just got home. They brought tons of food."

Hugh jumps up faster than Kaigo recovering from a hit, but Devesh still manages to push past him on the way to the kitchen.

Food? I don't know if it's my nerves about the tournament or this whole thing with Cali, but my stomach feels like it's taken a sucker punch and landed up near my throat. From the laptop the commentator says, "Looks like JStar's not happy with that loss." Oh, crap! This is the most embarrassing part. I wish Cali would go to the kitchen with the guys.

"You see that? Not even a handshake!"

"Only twelve years old. His lack of maturity is really showing here. No need to get all salty over this one, though. Both competitors advance to Top 16. We may get to see this matchup again tomorrow."

"Doesn't matter how old he is or how mad, he should shake hands. That's not cool."

I swallow. "He's right. That wasn't cool. Sorry." I've been saying that to Cali a lot today.

"It's okay," she says.

Things are still weird between us. The only way I can think of to fix it is to pretend like everything's normal. "You play a kickass Ylva."

"Thanks."

"When'd you start playing her?"

"Ever since she came out last year. I love her Super where she howls for moon power. I've been using her a lot lately, so that creep—Sage—wouldn't find me so easy."

"I'm sorry Mel's freaking you out about him."

"It's not Melanie. She's just looking out for me. She's the only one here who knows what it feels like to be a girl."

What can I say to that?

CHAPTER 22

Back in the little house, Ruby cries and cries. I finally give up on sleeping, grab the cookie bag from my backpack, and take three steps to the kitchen. They might not have much in the fridge, but there is no shortage of milk in this house. Most of it is in little jars. I open a carton and pour myself a glass.

Cali's laptop is on the kitchen table, so while I'm dunking cookies I scroll through the comments under our match again. The one from Ty and Flash is annoying. What's their problem?

There's a new comment under it:

Hailstorm: @Tygerflash U R way bigger losers than @JSTAR

Could that be Hailey? Is she actually watching Underground Hype? I want to write back to her, but what can I say? Thanks for kind of sticking up for me?

I keep scrolling to Sage's comment.

ShoMe: New outfit & imperio will rule stream TMRW
ShoMe: Shorter + Tighter = Better

I imagine how Cali would feel reading that. He's not talking about Cali's skills; it's all about her looks. Does anyone comment on my looks? Even when Devesh streams my fights, no one mentions that I'm a guy. Haters write things like, "What a loser to drop that combo." The worst I've gotten is some swear words or "You suck, stop playing." Now that I think of it, I'm surprised no one's ever commented on my hair. I've got some weird parts that always stick up.

I keep reading.

HYlo: @ShoMe: So tru I'd watch that
Baman: She can super me any day
Jumbolaya: Too young :(Look but don't touch LOL

"You can't sleep either?" I jump at the sound of Cali's voice. I didn't hear her coming with all the crying. I close the laptop. She sits in the chair across from me.

I push the cookie bag in her direction. There are only a couple left. "I don't know how you do it. The crying—it's like an infinity attack on my brain."

"You get used to it." She takes one.

"Really?"

"No."

We sit in what would be silence if Ruby wasn't howling. We used to hang out like this all the time. We had a Spy Club under our porch at home, and we'd sit in it forever without talking so no one would know we were there. Now, things are so weird between us, I feel like I have to fill the air with words.

"You like it here?" I ask.

"No."

Stupid question.

"I want to go home," she says. A tear rolls down her cheek, and with it comes a super-combo attack of complaints. "I miss my mom. I worry about her all the time. And my sister—I'm supposed to love her, but she's always screaming. And I can't sleep, like, ever. I've got no one to talk to. All my friends are back home. My dad ignores me. He ignores all of us. He thinks we're annoying. Marnie's nice, but she's always busy with Ruby. And then Sage sends me all those creepy messages. And my best friend thinks I'm making it all up."

Me? If I'm her best friend, I sure suck at it. No wonder Cali's been acting so crazy. I probably would too if I was dealing with all that.

"I'm sorry," I say again because I can't think of anything else and that's been working pretty good today.

"Geez, Jaden, I don't want you to be sorry. I need you to get it." She looks at me and sighs. "You have no idea what I'm talking about, do you?" She's a better best friend than I am. She knows me so well.

"It's like everything is different now that you're a girl," I say.

"I've always been a girl."

"I know, but it never mattered before." She wants me to get it, so I ask, "What's it like?"

"What?"

"Being a girl."

She squints her eyes at me.

"Before, you said Melanie's the only one around here who knows what it feels like."

She shrugs. "I don't know. It's hard to explain."

My turn to sigh.

After a minute she says, "Do you ever get a gross feeling, deep in your gut, when you're watching a scary movie?"

"Yeah."

"Well, that's the feeling I get when I read some of those comments. Remember that movie where the girl is on the phone with the psycho guy and then she finds out that the phone call is coming from inside the house?"

I nod.

"That's how I felt when ShoMe said he knows where I live. I mean, who says that? He must know that's scary. And I got that feeling around Sage yesterday too, even before I knew he was ShoMe. The way he looks at me and the stuff he says. Creeps me out."

"Wow."

"I knew you wouldn't understand."

"No, seriously. Wow. I had no idea." I look at her. "But you don't have to worry. We're all here to protect you if anyone ever does anything."

"That's exactly it. And I hate it."

"What?"

"What it feels like to be a girl. It's like . . . like you're never safe."

◄○►

We pass Ruby's room on our way back to bed. Marnie is sitting in a rocking chair holding the baby, whose crying is down to a light whimper. It's dark in the room, but I'm pretty sure both of them have their eyes closed. Cali carefully takes Ruby out of Marnie's arms. The baby turns up the volume long enough to wake Marnie, then quiets down again.

"Whatever you do, don't put her down," Marnie says.

"I know," Cali answers. "Go sleep. I'll hold her."

Marnie hesitates. "I should say no, but . . . I'm so tired." She gets up and Cali sits in the rocking chair. "Thank you."

I lie down on the floor of the dark room. As long as Ruby's not crying, I think I could fall asleep anywhere.

As I'm drifting off to sleep I hear Cali whispering, "It's okay, Ruby. You can do this. You're going to learn to sleep on your own. I know you will. You're strong like Ylva. You can do anything."

CHAPTER 23

In the morning I wake early on the floor of Ruby's room. At some point Marnie must have come back and taken Ruby again. I take a shower. When I peek into Cali's room I'm not surprised to see Mel still lying in bed. But I am surprised that Cali's not up. It's almost time to leave.

"I'm not going," she says.

"You have to. You made Top 16. That's huge."

"I never should have signed up for this tournament. I don't want to compete if it's going to mess us up. Anyway, I only made Top 16 because of you."

"No way. I had no chance against you playing Ylva. You slaughtered me."

She shakes her head. "You're just being nice."

"I wish. Seriously, you were fierce. Now get ready."

"It's okay, this is your thing."

"Nu-uh. You made Top 16. If you're not there, I'll always wonder if you would have won. And you will too." She doesn't make a move to get up. "Is this about Sage?"

She shrugs.

"Because you're not just fierce in the game, you know. You're fierce in real life too. That's what I lo— like about you." That was close; I almost said the other *L* word. "You handle all this stuff I never could. Like taking care of your mom and dealing with a baby."

She presses her lips together and looks down at her blanket. It doesn't look like I convinced her.

"You can take on the trash-talkers. Beat Sage and show him what a girl can do. Show everyone."

When she doesn't move, I hit her with my best shot. "I'm not going without you."

She gets up. "Fine," she says, and heads to the kitchen.

When she's gone, I grab Melanie's phone and dial.

"*Wei?*"

"*Ma ma?* It's me."

"*Er zi?* What are you wearing? *Jie jie* told me you lost your suitcase."

"Don't worry, Ma. I'm just wearing my jeans again. They gave me a shirt from ArcadeStix."

"But what about your underwear?"

She tells me to buy some new ones. Like I have time for that. I turn the conversation to something more important. "Ma, I think Cali should come home with us. Can you call her dad?"

Of course, it's not that simple. My mom has lots of questions. But this time I actually have some answers.

When I hang up, Melanie rolls over. Without opening her eyes she says, "Maybe you're not such a jerk after all."

—◦—

The rest of the team stayed at the hotel, so I'm the last one to get to our meeting at Chez Antoine again. Kyle nods at me from his seat at the head of the table, but he's deep in conversation with Jeffy and Nicco on either side of him. They all made the *Mega Haunt* Top 16.

The only seat left is at the other end of the table between Sage and Chung-Key.

Sage is sucking coffee through a fat lip. He looks like he just lost a battle with Kaigo. "Good morning," he says, but not like he means it.

I don't know what to think of Sage anymore. I remember his online comments about Cali, and what she said about him making her feel scared. Then I remember the help he gave me yesterday. He's the only one besides Kyle who's been nice to me from the beginning. Not like Chung-Key, who thinks I'm an annoying kid, or the other guys, who just ignore me. "You okay?" I ask.

Sage nods halfheartedly.

I look at Chung-Key. As usual, he's frowning. "We went out last night and someone"—he looks at Sage—"didn't know when to shut up."

"You got in a fight with the O team?" I ask, kind of freaked.

"Not O," Chung-Key says. "SaltyPeppa."

"Why? What'd you say?"

"Nothing your young ears should hear," Chung-Key says.

Kyle turns his attention to our *Cross Ups* end of the table. "Okay, guys. No more easy games. Everyone competing today earned their spot. Remember, it's double elimination now."

That's what the T3 tournament was like too. You get two chances. So, if you lose a game, you get knocked down to the losers' bracket; if you lose again, you're out.

Kyle goes on. "We've got four Os still in play, including that big mouth ORevoir. JStar, we filled you in a lot yesterday on how these guys play. But there are a couple of surprises out there, even another young unknown."

"Oh, that's She-Star's girl," Sage says.

"Seriously? Now it's your turn to fill us in," Kyle says.

I squirm. Do I even know? "Honestly, she played a whole different character and style yesterday. She changed everything up."

"Uh-oh! Better hope she's not looking to change up her boyfriend too!" Sage laughs.

"She's just a friend," I say. My best friend!

◄o►

Devesh and Hugh are at my first station before I am.

"Today we're going to watch all your matches," Devesh says. After what Cali said yesterday, I think they're scared to go near her.

My first game is against some guy from New York who calls himself 2Bad. Too bad for him, because I win in two games.

"How'd your first game go?" I ask Cali when we find her with Mel and Roy.

"I didn't play. The guy never showed up."

"Sweet!" Devesh says. "Automatic win."

"Not that you need it, of course," Hugh stammers.

"You guys need to relax," Melanie says.

I'm glad when I hear my name being called to station seven for my next match. I can see a neon-blue shirt there already. From a distance I can tell the guy's hair is too short to be ORevoir. I'm relieved, until we start playing. This guy, Odyssée, is godlike too. No wonder the O team is so cocky!

He mains Kaigo, so it's a mirror match. I dress my Kaigo in red for ArcadeStix and he dresses his in blue for O.

Odyssée plays a typical O rushdown style and I do my best to keep up. The match is total mayhem. Fireballs fly everywhere. Our dragons lock necks and swing each other around in crazy circles.

He lands a number of counterattacks that hit me while I'm using my bread-and-butter combo. Looks like I'm not the only one who did some research last night. He's ready when I make the mistakes the commentators pointed out.

My red Kaigo gets juggled and thrown to the ground a lot more than his blue Kaigo. The loss knocks me down to the losers' bracket.

I try not to freak out. At T3 I showed up late and missed my first game, so I played the entire tournament from the losers'. It was actually a good thing, because that's where the weaker players all end up. I can avoid the best of the best—at least for now.

Hugh comes running over, waving his paper in my face. "OMG, Jaden! Look who you're playing next!"

CHAPTER 24

I grab the paper out of Hugh's hand and try to read the names in the bracket he drew. He's been filling it out based on everyone's wins and losses. I think he has more information on here than the tournament organizers, if anyone could read it. His writing is so messy, I can't even find my name.

"You're *J*, for JStar. Here!" He points to what I thought was a *U*. Under it he's scribbled what looks like a *C*.

"Who's that? Cali?"

"No! She's *I* for Imperio."

"So is that an *O*? Which one?"

"An *O*? " Hugh points the paper at Devesh. "Does that look like an *O* to you?"

Devesh puts up his hands. "I can't read any of that."

"Just tell me who I'm playing."

"It's Chung-Key!"

I stare at Hugh. "But . . . how'd he get into losers?"

"He lost to one of the guys from the O team," Hugh explains. "Ohlala."

This is not good. No matter who wins this game, ArcadeStix will be down one player in the tournament. Chung-Key's words from yesterday loop in my head. "Don't make us look stupid for having a kid on our team."

If I lose he'll be mad.

But I'm pretty sure he'll be even madder if I win.

A few minutes later I sit at the station, thumbs tapping my controller like crazy.

Cali slumps down beside me in the empty seat. Turns out she lost her match too.

"Don't worry, you guys," Hugh says. "It's not over yet."

"I know," Cali says.

"Of course you know. I was just, like, giving you a pep talk . . ." Hugh can't talk fast enough. "Which of course you don't nee—"

I cut him off. "Who's she playing next?"

Hugh consults his crumpled paper. "2Bad."

"I played him. He was nothing special," I say. "He played Cantu and he likes his space. Just keep pressuring him into the corner. He hates that. He'll take risks to get past you and you can punish him."

"Okay. Thanks," she says.

Chung-Key shows up and Cali gets up to give him the seat. His eyes, nose, and mouth are all frowning as he shakes my hand. "Teammates or not, every man for himself," he says.

"Uh, okay." Could he be any more intimidating?

He selects his main, Blaze, and the *FIGHT!* sign flashes.

The first round ends with a Dragon Breath

Super—I blow flames on him until he ignites. The second round finishes when he launches an infinite attack of fiery feathers at me.

We go round for round, burning each other up. The screen is blazing red and orange.

We're still tied when it comes to the third round of game three. Whoever loses is out of the tournament.

FIGHT!

Just as I launch into my first attack I hear, "Go, *She-Star*!" Crap! Why's that ORevoir guy cheering for me?

I jump over Chung-Key, because I've noticed that he's weak on the cross ups, which is funny since that's the name of this game. I get an eight-kick combo in before he puts his block up.

"Bravo, *She-Star*!"

"How do you say 'shut up' in French?" I ask Chung-Key.

Chung-Key gives a quick snort, then transforms Blaze into a phoenix and starts flinging feathers at me again. I transform too, and use my Dragon Fire Super to spin across the screen in a cloud of smoke.

Our health bars are still even. We go punch for punch, kick for kick, and flame for flame. This round might time out. That means whoever has more health when the timer hits zero wins. I need to make sure that's me.

I jump over him again, and get more kicks in from behind.

"That's the way, *She-Star*." ORevoir counts down with the timer. "*Dix, neuf, huit . . .*"

I get in a string of punches and then one more of my go-to combo just as he gets to *un*. It's so close we have to wait for the screen to tell us who won. Please! Please! Please!

KAIGO WINS!!

Chung-Key rips his controller plug out, kind of like I did after playing Cali yesterday. But unlike me, he shakes hands swiftly before he stomps off.

ORevoir calls, "*Merci, She-Star!*"

Thank you? Oh, now it makes sense. He wanted me to win so Chung-Key would be eliminated. He's not so tough after all. He's actually scared to play Chung-Key.

"You won't be thanking me after I take you down," I say.

CHAPTER 25

I'm surprised when I turn around and see Sage waiting for me after my next game.

"Ready for another business lunch?" he asks.

What do I say? He's my teammate. I see Hugh, Devesh, and Cali watching me, like they don't know what I'm going to say either. "Um, no thanks. I'm gonna have lunch with my friends today."

"They can sit in," he says. "I don't mind helping your girlfriend out, She-Star."

"I told you, she's not my girlfriend," I say, loud enough for Cali to hear. "And stop calling me that."

"Okay, chillax," Sage says. "Just trying to help."

Did I take it too far? I steal a line from Melanie. "It's just . . . we have plans." I head over to my friends and the four of us walk to Mr. Burger.

I'm not sure where Melanie and Roy are. I haven't seen them in a while, but I'm sure Melanie will find me next time Mom calls.

With just the four of us, it's almost like old times—we eat and talk and no one says the word *girlfriend*.

Cali's the one giving me tournament advice now. "You need to stop letting that ORevoir guy get to you," she says.

She's got a lot more experience with this kind of thing than I do. "How?"

"Ignore him."

"Have you heard this guy? He doesn't shut up."

"Sometimes I just pretend I'm my character."

I think about that. When my Kaigo side takes over, I'm fierce too.

She goes on. "Ylva would never let anyone tell her who she is. Mean words just float past her in the wind, and she doesn't care."

Kaigo is a man of few words; he talks with his fists. To be like him, I need to let my game play speak for itself.

◄○►

Kyle gives me the same advice in his pep talk before the match.

"Don't react. It's unprofessional. Just stay quiet and let him run his mouth. Act like you don't even hear him. Remember, you represent ArcadeStix, so you need to behave respectably."

That must be why Chung-Key never said anything back to ORevoir during their match.

I'm glad this fight isn't being streamed. I plug in and my thumbs tap the buttons on my controller.

When ORevoir shows up, his long hair is in a ponytail, like he means business. He starts into the trash talk before he's even plugged in. "I'm happy you beat Chung-Key." He pronounces *happy* without the *h*. "Much easier for me now."

It's really hard not to say something rude back because this guy reminds me of Ty and Flash. Staying silent just makes him try harder.

"Soon you can go home to your *maman, She-Star,*" ORevoir says. "Little boys don't win big-boy money."

I look at Kyle but he just shakes his head.

"Oh, is Kyle your *maman*?"

"Hey, ease up."

I know that voice, but I have to turn and look because I never expected to hear it defend me.

CHAPTER 26

"You?" ORevoir says, pointing to Chung-Key. "Aren't you eliminated? Why are you even here?"

I'm wondering the same thing.

"I'm here for my team."

"You're wasting your time. Your team is pathetic. Today you lose to this little boy. *She-Star* lose to a little girl yesterday. And I hear"—his *hear* sounds like *ear* with the French accent—"last night a big girl beat up ShoMe."

The look on Kyle's face tells me that last part is news to him.

ORevoir bends down so he's right in my face. His breath smells like coffee. He talks to me like I'm three. "I understand if you want to give up and go home to your *maman*."

Kyle's sticking to his plan to ignore the trash talk. Easy for him—no one's calling him a baby. And

Chung-Key, the guy who said he's here for the team, walks away. I guess he'd rather go watch his other teammate battle. What did I expect?

I want to look ORevoir in the eye, but I'm pretty sure if I do I'll start crying. This weekend has turned out way worse than I could ever have imagined. I lost my controller and my confidence, and everything's turned weird with my best friend. Plus, I'm so tired from Ruby crying all night again. He's right. What chance do I have against all these pro gamers? I actually do want to go home to my mom. But I can't.

Suddenly, I realize: this must be what Cali feels like.

I can't stall forever. I press the Start button and do my best. ORevoir plays Goyle like a pro. While I'm playing it safe and defensive, he fills his meter by taunting me. He stands there with his hand on his hip looking at his pretend watch. Then his Lion Roar Super blows me off the screen. Before I'm out of hit-stun, he's on the attack, with a twelve-hit combo.

K.O.

I turn around. Chung-Key is back, and he's got one of those guys in the yellow STAFF shirts with him.

"You want your *maman* now, don't you, *She-Star*? Little boys all want their *maman* when they are scared."

"Back off," Chung-Key says.

"Now you are playing *maman* to this little boy who just kicked you out of the tournament?"

Chung-Key pulls ORevoir by the shoulder and turns him around. "He's not a little boy. He's my teammate, JStar. Learn to say it right!"

For a second, I think Chung-Key is going to hit ORevoir. But Kyle grabs him by the arm and pulls him away.

"Too bad," Hugh whispers. "If ORevoir got into a fight, he'd get disqualified for sure."

Round two looks a lot like round one, except faster.

When the *K.O.* flashes, ORevoir turns to me. "See? I will decimate you." He runs his finger along his neck again, like cutting someone's throat.

I swallow and try not to cry. Why am I letting this guy's words freak me out? It's just trash talk, right? I'm used to that.

Behind him I see Chung-Key pointing at ORevoir and talking angrily to the STAFF guy. All his frowns really emphasize his words. The guy in the STAFF shirt steps forward. "ORevoir, this is a warning," he says. "You need to back off. You can't threaten your competitors. If you continue, you'll be asked to leave and be disqualified."

Cali calls out from behind me. "C'mon, Jaden!" I remember how she said she pretends to be Ylva. I need to be Kaigo now.

I press Start and the *FIGHT!* sign flashes.

Of all the players I studied last night, I spent the most time watching ORevoir. He's good, and he knows it. But he's also cocky and he loves to play his taunts to get the crowd going.

I purposely whiff some basic moves to give him a sense of confidence. If he thinks I play like a little boy, I'm going to use that to my advantage. Just as I expected, he plays a taunt, standing there with his arms open wide. Thank you! I go in for the punish—a fourteen-hit combo followed by my Dragon Fire Super ends the round.

ORevoir may be cocky, but he's no fool. He stops taunting and Lion Roars and Eagle Claws me to pieces to win the match.

ORevoir holds out his hand for a fist bump. When I hesitate, he says, "You know I was only messing with you, right? Sorry if I went too far.

I don't mean to scare you, JStar." He actually pronounces it right.

"I wasn't scared," I say, and meet his fist bump with more force than needed.

I didn't win the match, and I'm out of the tournament. Sometimes your best isn't enough in *Cross Ups*—just like in real life. At least I got some respect.

"Now Sage is the last ArcadeStix player," Devesh says.

Hugh finishes marking up his paper. "And he's playing Cali next."

CHAPTER 27

"You have to admit, this is weird," I say. We're sitting in the front row, waiting for Cali's match against Sage to start.

"Which part?" Devesh asks. "The part where Cali is about to play her stalker or the part where you're wearing the same T-shirt as him?"

"Do you really think Sage is a stalker?"

"Nah. Jokes. The guy probably has no idea that Cali is freaked out by what he said. He's trying to be friendly and she's taking it the wrong way."

"Yeah. He's cool," Hugh says. "If he doesn't realize what he's saying to Cali is scaring her then he's not a jerk, he's just dumb."

"That's what I thought, but Cali's convinced he's a creep."

"So, you and Cali have conflicting hypotheses," Hugh says.

"You guys spent too much time at STEM Camp," Devesh says.

"But which one of us is right?" I ask.

"Dude!" Hugh is super excited. "You could do an experiment to test your hypothesis!"

Devesh snorts. "You want to do an experiment to see if Sage is dumb?"

"Sort of," Hugh says.

"Hey, Sage, what's the square root of one-forty-four?" Devesh chuckles.

"I don't care if he's good at math," I say. "I need to figure out if he knows he crossed the line with those messages. I have an idea."

I need to talk to Cali fast, before the match starts. I race up onto the stage. Sage and Cali are already set up, waiting for the commentators to announce their match. I need to tell Cali my plan, without Sage knowing. The only thing I can think of is to speak to her in Mandarin. It's weird. Even though we both speak Mandarin to our moms, I've never spoken it to her.

"*Xin Yi.*" I use her Chinese name. "Don't take this the wrong way, but in case you need an advantage . . . you should say—"

"No coaching allowed. Step off the stage," the announcer says on his way up the steps.

I look at Cali, then out to the crowd. "I'm just wishing her good luck," I say.

Cali is staring at me. "Say what?" she asks in Mandarin.

I bend down to give her a kiss on the cheek so I can whisper in her ear. This is not going to help with the rumors. Then I get off the stage as fast as I can.

"What did you tell her?" the guys ask.

I wave them off. I want to watch, not talk.

I'm surprised when Sage selects Kaigo. I didn't expect him to main the same guy I do. Cali wavers, then selects Ylva, the dire wolf she used to beat me.

Sage plays Kaigo like a beast. I'm glad I don't have to go up against him. He sticks to basic combos, obviously baiting her to take risks. But she's patient.

She comes at him with a slide attack, her leg outstretched. He goes down and she jumps on him, getting in a seven-kick combo. He grabs her and they tumble along the ground. He breathes fire in her direction, and I'm amazed when she gets out of the way in time.

She's keeping up with Sage. And yesterday she beat MrWinDoh and an O player. And she's doing it all with that little black gamepad. This is a way bigger tournament than my first one. No wonder Devesh won't shut up about how good she is.

The first round goes to Sage, but just barely. Cali leans over to him and says something.

"Thought she was too scared to talk to him," Devesh says.

"She's using my plan," I say. Then I remember: that's my teammate she's using it against.

And it's working. The next round Cali is all over Sage. He whiffs his next three attacks. Cali howls to the moon and shoots sparkling yellow beams from her dire wolf's eyes. She's right: it really does look cool, almost cooler than the Dragon Fire Super that Sage is using now. But it isn't enough. Cali only needs one quick cross up. She sinks her canines into his neck and Sage is K.O.

"Look, she's talking to him again," Devesh says.

"What did you tell her?" Hugh begs. "She's freaking him out, big time."

He's right. Sage is totally off his game now. Moves that he completed no problem in round one, he can't finish. Cali doesn't need to be patient anymore. She goes ham on screen. Uppercut, flying side kick, Wolf Claw Super. On and on it goes. She wins the next three rounds easy, finishing with a Wolf Tail Super that swipes him right off the screen.

Ylva's win quote flashes onto the screen:

STAND UP AND DEFEND YOURSELF!

Cali makes her way down the stage steps.

Melanie and Roy emerge from the crowd and swallow her in a hug.

"You were godlike!" Devesh says when she gets to us. "Or should I say goddesslike?"

"What did you say to him?" Hugh asks.

"She told him she's HermIone," I say proudly.

"You what?" Melanie screeches.

"Not exactly," Cali says. "I'm not stupid. I told him I know what he's been writing to HermIone. Then I told him she's only twelve, and if he doesn't stop I'm telling the police."

"What did he say?" Hugh asks.

"Not one word."

My stomach drops. Cali just proved her own hypothesis. Sage is a creep. He knows what he's doing is wrong. His actions spoke for him.

Sage comes off the stage and blows right past us. He doesn't get far before Kyle and Chung-Key stop him and wave me over.

I grab Cali's hand. Devesh and Hugh follow us.

When we get to the Arcade Stix group, Kyle says, "I know you're not happy that all three of you are eliminated already. I'm surprised too. I thought for sure we'd have a rep in the finals. But you all made Top 16, so this was still a strong outing for the team."

As soon as there's a pause I say, "Thanks for this opportunity, Kyle, but I quit the team."

CHAPTER 28

Mouths drop open.

"What are you talking about?" Kyle says.

"I can't be on a team with him." I point to Sage. "He just admitted he's been trolling girls online."

Sage shakes his head. "I didn't know she was twelve."

"It doesn't matter how old she is, man. You're messed up." I shake my head.

Kyle jumps in. "Whoa! Whoa! What are you saying? Sage, are you admitting to creeping girls online?"

"It's not just online," Chung-Key says. "He got punched last night by SaltyPeppa for coming on too strong."

"Sage, man," Kyle says. "You're the one who's off the team. We can't have someone representing us who's out there harassing people like that."

"Are you kidding me? I made it farther than either of these guys today." Sage points to Chung-Key and me.

"True. But you didn't beat this rising star." Kyle turns to Cali. "Sorry, I only know you as Imperio."

"That tag was just for today. My name's Cali."

"Nice to meet you, Cali. I've been watching you play today and you're not just impressive, you're godlike. I notice you play with a gamepad, like Jaden used to. I'd love to see what happens to your game with our product." He glances at Sage. "Since we have an opening on our team, I'd like to invite you to join us. You'll get an ArcadeStix controller and we'll pay your entrance and travel for tournaments."

"You're serious?" Sage says.

"Very," Kyle answers.

"You're making a big mistake." Sage walks off.

"Don't worry about him. We need people who represent us well."

"I don't know if I'm going to do any more tournaments—" Cali starts, then her name is called over the speakers for her next match.

"Go," Kyle says. "We can talk more later, Cali. Good luck!"

"You've got this!" I call after her as she heads to her station. Then I look at Chung-Key. "You would be okay with that?" I ask. "Being on a team with two kids?"

"Hell ya!" he says and breaks into a smile. "If they play like you two!" He gives me a fist bump. "But seriously. That was a stand-up move just now. Cali's a lucky girl."

"She's not my girlfriend," I say.

"Well, then she's lucky to have a friend like you."

For the first time in a while, I think that's true.

It turns out Cali's next game is against ORevoir. They're on stream, so he doesn't do any trash-talking. Probably worried about getting DQ'd.

Cali plays Ylva versus his Goyle. And that's what they look like sitting up on the stage. She's tiny next to ORevoir. But she's fierce. So fierce that he doesn't even taunt her once. He doesn't get a chance, she's moving so fast. She swipes at him with Wolf Claws from the front, then she's up and over him, kicking him from behind. When he turns she knocks him off his lion paws with her powerful tail. Then she's on top, getting in a fifteen-hit combo.

She takes the first two rounds with supersonic speed, each one ending with moon lasers jetting from her eyes into Goyle's giant chest.

Then ORevoir figures her out. His rushdown style with big, bulky Goyle is no match against her tiny speed demon. So, he becomes a turtle. He stops attacking and blocks like mad until she gets frustrated. He waits for solid openings before throwing any moves. When Cali jumps over him he grabs her, spins her like a pizza, and slams her down.

K.O.

He takes all of the next rounds. The match ends like the last fight in the *Karate Kid* movie. ORevoir rises up onto his lion legs and kicks Cali in the head with Goyle's Eagle Strike Super. Except, instead of one blow to the face, there are, like, fifty. And instead of the good guy winning, it's ORevoir.

Cali shakes his hand with her head held high. "Good game."

"You are strong player. Very . . . how you say, *féroce*." He makes a clawing motion with his hand.

"Thank you," she says.

When she gets down the stage steps, I give her a high ten. "You are amazing!" We both know I'm not just talking about the tournament.

Devesh says, "That was awesome."

"Totally amazeballs, dude!" Hugh says.

Cali smiles the biggest smile I've seen since I got to Montreal.

"Tell her the good news!" Melanie says.

Mom called halfway through the match. "You're coming home with us tomorrow!" I say.

I don't know if it's because of the good news or because of how well she did at the tournament, but Cali's eyes sparkle super bright—I can practically see yellow moonbeams shooting out of them. I like looking into her eyes, but they don't make me feel like jelly inside, like Hailey's green-gray eyes do. Cali's eyes just feel like . . . home.

ORevoir goes on to win Underground Hype. I figure that when you get kicked out by the guy who wins the whole tournament, it's basically like coming in second. So you could say me and Cali tied.

CHAPTER 29

At the train station Monday morning Cali has two big suitcases to pull while the rest of us only have backpacks. I wonder how she packed so fast. When she was moving to Montreal it took her forever.

Marnie drove us, since Cali's dad had to work. She passes Ruby to me so she can take one of Cali's suitcases.

"I can take a suitcase," I say, trying to hand the baby back.

"It's good for Ruby to be in someone else's arms once in a while," Marnie says.

I wonder why those other arms are never her father's. It's daytime, so Ruby is fast asleep. She's actually kind of cute.

When we get to the right platform, Cali looks at Ruby in my arms and says, "If only she would do that at night."

"She will, eventually," Marnie says.

"I remember holding you like that when you were a baby," Melanie says to me.

"Really?" I ask. She's only four years older than me.

"Oh yeah! You were like Ruby. Crying all the time. Sometimes Mom needed a break."

"Well, they say it takes a village to raise a baby," Marnie says.

"Why doesn't Dad do any of the baby stuff?" Cali asks.

"You know, he works all day," Marnie says.

"But you work all day *and* all night," Cali says. "You need a break too."

"Aren't you sweet."

We see Devesh, Hugh, and Roy walking toward us as the train pulls into the station.

Marnie says, "Oh, I'm going to miss you, sweetie." There are tears in her eyes. "Say hi to your mom from us. I hope she's well and you can get back to your normal life. But you're always welcome here. You know that, right?"

"Thanks"—Cali gives Marnie a hug—"for everything." Then she comes over to me and strokes Ruby's hair. "Be strong, sis." She leans down and gives the baby a kiss on the forehead.

I hand Ruby back and grab one of Cali's suitcases to drag onto the train. I wonder if I'll ever see my lost suitcase again. I had to give the arcade stick Kyle loaned me back after the tournament, and there's no way I can afford to buy a new one.

◄o►

This time we find an empty section and get four seats together. Me and Cali sit facing Devesh and Hugh with a table in the middle. Melanie and Roy sit across the aisle from us.

Hugh pulls out a pack of cards and starts shuffling. "It's so cool you're going to be on the ArcadeStix team now," he says to Cali.

"I don't know," Cali says. "I'm not sure about doing more tournaments."

"C'mon, you have to," I say.

"Yeah!" Devesh says. "You'll be so famous. Jaden already gets tons of attention for being the youngest player at tournaments. You've got the bonus of being a girl. I mean, there are hardly any girl players. You're a hot ticket. Probably worth as much as Yuudai Sato. You could make good money!"

"I just want to play for fun," Cali says.

Hugh deals the cards. "Why can't you have fun *and* make money?"

"Please," I beg. "It'll be more fun with you there."

"I'll talk to my mom about it," she says.

"I wish I was a girl," Devesh says. "I bet more people would watch my stream."

"You think people would take you seriously? They act like girls can't know anything about fighting games," Cali says.

"I didn't say they'd take me seriously. I said I'd get more views," Devesh says.

"Trust me, you don't want those people watching."

We play a million rounds of the card game President. Cali spends most of the time as president.

"Are you guys letting me win?" she asks.

"Definitely not," Devesh says. "We learned our lesson."

"You're just getting all the good cards," Hugh says.

I hope this is a sign of better things to come for Cali.

Meanwhile, I keep ending up as the scum—the last player to play all his cards. Feels like a good fit after this weekend.

◄O►

Mom is standing on the platform twisting her jade bracelet around her wrist the way she does when she's worried. Dad and Josh are there too.

We all get off the train except Roy, who hangs back. I guess he's waiting for us to clear the platform.

"I'm so happy you are all back safe," Mom says, giving Cali a hug, then me.

"We're fine, *Ma*," I say, pushing out of her bear hug.

"Your mom was worried about you all weekend," Dad says, leaning in for his own hug.

"I can't believe you lost your suitcase. Loser."
Josh shakes his head.

"What happened to it? Devesh said the bomb
squad would blow it up. Is my controller okay?"

"Sorry." Josh pops his hands open and makes an
explosion sound.

My heart sinks.

He laughs.

"He's just joking," Dad says. "The rail company
called and we picked it up from the Lost and Found
yesterday. Your precious controller is at home waiting for you."

"Right next to my latest MVP trophy," Josh adds,
and punches me in the arm.

I breathe out. My controller is safe. It's no tournament win, but today it feels like a victory.

On Tuesday, Cali comes to STEM Camp with me.
Mom thinks it's a good idea for her to get to know
my school.

Hugh isn't sitting alone when we arrive.

"I thought you didn't want to come to science
camp," I say to Devesh. We all know he's more
interested in Cali than science.

"I tried to call you guys yesterday to tell you I signed up," he says.

"We were at the rehab center visiting Cali's mom."

"How's she doing?" he asks Cali.

She smiles. "Actually, really good. Her cast is off and she's walking okay. She needs to get stronger and practice stairs now."

"So, you'll be coming to Layton in September?" Devesh leans back, trying to act all casual. His big smile gives him away.

"Hope so," Cali says.

We spend the morning experimenting with magnets, seeing how they attract and repel each other. Kind of like Devesh and Cali.

After lunch we head out to the field. The Sports Leadership Camp is already there.

"Look!" Ty yells. "Jaden brought his girlfriend from Montreal."

"Cali?" Tanaka says. "You're back!"

It turns out Tanaka and Cali know each other. They sit together.

"What happened? Did she dump you after she beat you?" Ty says.

"I bet she was never his girlfriend," Flash says. "He's a fraud."

I channel my inner Kaigo and remain silent.

But Cali channels her inner Ylva. "I hear you're the fraud," she says.

There's a chorus of oohs and someone yells, "Roasted!"

Then Mr. Efram claps to get everyone's attention. He explains how a compass works and how to read one. "Today you'll practice navigating with a compass. With a partner, you'll follow these directions to find the clue boxes hidden around the schoolyard. In the last box, there's a prize!"

At the word *partner*, Tanaka and Cali hold hands. Hugh and Devesh partner up. I look at Hailey. Her green-gray eyes meet mine. Do I dare? Maybe I'm better off asking a little kid.

"Come on, JStar," she says. I follow her to get a compass and clue sheet from Mr. Efram. Once we're off by ourselves in the field, I can't resist asking, "Did you . . . was that you . . . are you Hailstorm?"

"Yeah." She looks down.

She watched me play! What does that mean? If I've learned anything from this weekend in Montreal, maybe I should start with the obvious question. "Do you play *Cross Ups*?"

"Totally." As we go from clue to clue I find out she's a serious gamer. She mains Ylva, because, just like Cali, she loves the Moon Howl Super. She knows me from watching me play on stream and we've even played online before. I just never knew because I used to think all gamers are guys. I don't tell her that. I want her to get to know the new, improved me.

"Do you know how to get Ylva to focus her moonbeam?" she asks.

Ugh. I don't know the answer. What do I say? "Well, you have to . . . I think you need to . . . talk to Cali. She plays a fierce Ylva."

"Okay," she says. "So, is she your girlfriend?"

"She's a girl and she's my friend."

"Just a friend?"

I feel Kaigo's heat on my cheeks. "No, not just a friend. She's my best friend."

ACKNOWLEDGMENTS

To the talented members of my critique group—Karen Cole, Heather Tucker, Sandra Clarke, Patrick Meade, Anne MacLachlan, and Steve Chatterton: thank you for loving Jaden and helping me guide him through the cross ups of life.

The Writers' Community of Durham Region has been a great support, helping me gain knowledge and friendships through writing. Particular thanks to the three brave members who answered my call for a super-last-minute beta read—Naomi Mesbur, Barbara Hunt, and Caroline McIntosh.

The Fighting Game Community (FGC) in Toronto has been open and helpful to me whenever I attend tournaments. Thanks to Nicholas Victoria of Basement Gaming for answering random questions about tournament structure and rules. Special thanks to Michelle van Trang (Starmie G), Jacqueline Manor (Jakyo Manor), Rebecca Boudreault (Becca Blade), and Samantha M. (Toffee) for taking the time to share their perspectives about the female experience in the FGC.

Thank you to my agent, Amy Tompkins, and the team at Annick Press, especially my editor, Katie Hearn, and the talented Connie Choi who brings Jaden and his friends to life on the page.

Growing up, I never doubted I could do anything I set my mind to. That was because I had amazing parents who always supported me. Thank you, Mom and Dad!

Finally, thank you to my husband and daughters for your support and . . . everything. I love you.

Sylv Chiang is a middle grade teacher by day and a writer of middle grade fiction by night. She lives in Pickering, Ontario.

 Connie Choi graduated from the bachelor of illustration program at Sheridan College. She lives in Toronto, Ontario.

WATCH FOR BOOK 3
IN THE **CROSS UPS** SERIES

RISING STAR

SYLV CHIANG

Art by **CONNIE CHOI**

 Coming in Fall 2019!

 annick press
toronto + berkeley

CHAPTER 1

"Finally!" From the sidewalk I see two UPS boxes sitting side by side at our front doors. I turn to high-five Cali, but she's already taking off.

I scramble behind her up our steep porch steps and use my house key to tear open the tape on my box. "Yes!" I hold up my advance copy of *Cross Ups V* in victory.

"C'mon." She grabs the key from my hand and opens my door while I rip the plastic off the game.

We drop our backpacks, jump out of our shoes, and run to the living room. Lights are all off, so I know I'm home first. Instruction papers fall to the floor. Who needs those? I grab the disk and slide it in.

"It's beautiful," she says. We're staring at the picture on the box, waiting for the start-up screen

1

to appear on my TV. It shows all the characters around a giant *V* because this is the fifth version of *Cross Ups*.

"Look at Kaigo!" I say. My main, a big muscly guy, has a new spiky hairstyle and more badges on his kung fu uniform. I wish I looked like him. I'm the scrawniest guy in grade eight.

"Who's that?" Cali points to a woman with a long, black ponytail that starts right above her forehead.

"Who cares? Let's go." I click through to select the new Kaigo and start a match. "This is amazing." My thumbs tap the controller buttons excitedly. Ever since the announcement that Cross Ups was releasing a new game, it's been all I can think about. And the graphics totally live up to the hype. The new Kaigo looks so crisp. And the colors are different—his dragon side is brighter green now. Everything looks so high def.

Cali's playing Ylva, the dire wolf–cross. Her cavewoman outfit is different, too—shorter and striped.

I go for a Dragon Fire Super, my hardest move, but whiff. She uses my mistake to grab me and spin me over her head.

The home phone rings. Yes, we still have a land-line. My mom is stuck in the last century. She won't even let me have a cellphone.

"You gonna get that?" Cali asks, her on-screen-self pouncing on me as soon as I recover.

"Nah, it's just Devesh or Hugh calling to see if it came. They've been calling every day since I told them about the advance copies." Cali and I are sponsored by ArcadeStix to play *Cross Ups*. Our rep, Kyle, sent us these advance copies of the new version so we can get our skills upped fast. He told me to keep it on the down low because the game doesn't actually come out for two more weeks, but of course I told my friends.

"You should really pick up. Could be Hailey."

"And let you say you won the first match on *V*? Nu-uh."

"So *Cross Ups Five* is more important than true love?" I know Cali's just going for the win because she never teases me about Hailey.

"Shut up." I try a Dragon Breath Super, but Kaigo doesn't transform into his dragon side and spin across the screen like he's supposed to. Okay, that's weird. I never miss that move. Why isn't

Kaigo responding right? Cali's not having any problem with her Supers. She howls to transform into a canine beast and shoots shimmering moonbeams at me from her eyes. I crumple to the ground.

As soon as I'm out of hit stun I try again. This time I input Dragon Tail Super.

Nothing.

What the? I've heard of characters playing differently in newer versions of a game. Am I going to have to relearn everything?

Cali's got me in a headlock. My face is turning blue and my Health Meter's almost empty.

The phone stops ringing and the answering machine—yes, we seriously still have one of those, too—picks up. After a few seconds where the outgoing message must be playing, we hear: "Hi, Jaden. It's Kyle. Listen, a great opportunity has come up. Give me a call . . ."

I jump off the couch, sending my huge controller thumping to the carpet. I get tangled in the cord and land on my knees. Then I'm up again, lunging at the phone, which falls to the ground. When I finally get it to my ear, I hear my screechy voice through the machine. "Kyle. I'm here."

Dead air on the other end of the receiver.

"What do you think that was about?" I ask Cali.

"Dunno. But I just kicked your butt."

This isn't the first time Cali's beat me. But it still burns. On screen, Ylva celebrates, shaking her hands wildly above her head. Her win quote runs along the bottom:

STAND UP AND DEFEND YOURSELF!

I wish I could. Will ArcadeStix even want me to represent them if I play *Cross Ups V* like this?